Crime By Gaslight, Volume 1

We all love a good crime story. An anthology of short crime stories, written by the finest of craftsman of their age, is always a welcome treat.

The short story is often viewed as an inferior relation to the Novel. But it is an art in itself. To take a story and distil its essence into fewer pages while keeping character and plot rounded and driven is not an easy task. Many try and many fail.

In this series we have a selection of short stories from many of our most accomplished writers written at the beginnings of Detective fiction.

Their art in writing a short story is sometimes barely noticed by a reader - such is the quality with which they are written. It is a difficult trade, an unforgiving discipline, but for those who master it, the rewards are many. Couple this with a time when crime and villainy were rife, when life was for those in the wrong class was difficult and you have the makings of a heady and exciting brew.

Index Of Contents

The Return Of Imray by Rudyard Kipling
The Eye Of Apollo by GK Chesterton
The Adventure Of The Copper Beeches by Arthur Conan Doyle
The Black Doctor by Arthur Conan Doyle
The Bolted Door by Edith Wharton
The Gerrard Street Mystery by John Charles Dent

The Return Of Imray by Rudyard Kipling

The doors were wide, the story saith,
Out of the night came the patient wraith,
He might not speak, and he could not stir
A hair of the Baron's minniver
Speechless and strengthless, a shadow thin,
He roved the castle to seek his kin.
And oh,'twas a piteous thing to see
The dumb ghost follow his enemy!
THE BARON.

Imray achieved the impossible. Without warning, for no conceivable motive, in his youth, at the threshold of his career he chose to disappear from the world, which is to say, the little Indian station where he lived.

Upon a day he was alive, well, happy, and in great evidence among the billiard-tables at his Club. Upon a morning, he was not, and no manner of search could make sure where he might be. He had stepped out of his place; he had not appeared at his office at the proper time, and his dogcart was not upon the public roads. For these reasons, and because he was hampering, in a microscopical degree, the administration of the Indian Empire, that Empire paused for one microscopical moment to make inquiry into the fate of Imray. Ponds were dragged, wells were plumbed, telegrams were despatched down the lines of railways and to the nearest seaport town-twelve hundred miles away; but Imray was not at the end of the drag-ropes nor the telegraph wires. He was gone, and his place knew him no more.

Then the work of the great Indian Empire swept forward, because it could not be delayed, and Imray from being a man became a mystery, such a thing as men talk over at their tables in the Club for a month, and then forget utterly. His guns, horses, and carts were sold to the highest bidder. His superior officer wrote an altogether absurd letter to his mother, saying that Imray had unaccountably disappeared, and his bungalow stood empty.

After three or four months of the scorching hot weather had gone by, my friend Strickland, of the Police, saw fit to rent the bungalow from the native landlord. This was before he was engaged to Miss Youghal, an affair which has been described in another place, and while he was pursuing his investigations into native life. His own life was sufficiently peculiar, and men complained of his manners and customs. There was always food in his house, but there were no regular times for meals. He ate, standing up and walking about, whatever he might find at the sideboard, and this is not good for human beings. His domestic equipment was limited to six rifles, three shot-guns, five saddles, and a collection of stiff-jointed mahseer-rods, bigger and stronger than the largest salmon-rods. These occupied one-half of his bungalow, and the other half was given up to Strickland and his dog Tietjens, an enormous Rampur slut who devoured daily the rations of two men. She spoke to Strickland in a language of her own; and whenever, walking abroad, she saw things calculated to destroy the peace of Her Majesty the Queen- Empress, she returned to her master and laid information. Strickland would take steps at once, and the end of his labours was trouble and fine and imprisonment for other people. The natives believed that Tietjens was a familiar spirit, and treated her with the great reverence that is born of hate and fear. One room in the bungalow was set apart for her special use. She owned a bedstead, a blanket, and a drinking- trough, and if any one came into Strickland's room at night her custom was to knock down the invader and give tongue till some one came with a light. Strickland owed his life to her, when he was on the Frontier, in search of a local murderer, who came in the gray dawn to send Strickland much farther than the Andaman Islands. Tietjens caught the man as he was crawling into Strickland's tent with a dagger between his teeth; and after his record of iniquity was established in the eyes of the law he was hanged. From that date Tietjens wore a collar of rough silver, and employed a monogram on her night-blanket; and the blanket was of double woven Kashmir cloth, for she was a delicate dog.

Under no circumstances would she be separated from Strickland; and once, when he was ill with fever, made great trouble for the doctors, because she did not know how to help her master and would not allow another creature to attempt aid. Macarnaght, of the Indian Medical Service, beat her over her head with a gun-butt before she could understand that she must give room for those who could give quinine.

A short time after Strickland had taken Imray's bungalow, my business took me through that Station, and naturally, the Club quarters being full, I quartered myself upon Strickland. It was a desirable bungalow, eight-roomed and heavily thatched against any chance of leakage from rain. Under the pitch of the roof ran a ceiling-cloth which looked just as neat as a white-washed ceiling. The landlord had repainted it when Strickland took the bungalow. Unless you knew how Indian bungalows were built you would never have suspected that above the cloth lay the dark three-cornered cavern of the roof, where the beams and the underside of the thatch harboured all manner of rats, bats, ants, and foul things.

Tietjens met me in the verandah with a bay like the boom of the bell of St. Paul's, putting her paws on my shoulder to show she was glad to see me. Strickland had contrived to claw together a sort of meal which he called lunch, and immediately after it was finished went out about his business. I was left alone with Tietjens and my own affairs. The heat of the summer had broken up and turned to the warm damp of the rains. There was no motion in the heated air, but the rain fell like ramrods on the earth, and flung up a blue mist when it splashed back. The bamboos, and the custard-apples, the poinsettias, and the mango-trees in the garden stood still while the warm water lashed through them, and the frogs began to sing among the aloe hedges. A little before the light failed, and when the rain was at its worst, I sat in the back verandah and heard the water roar from the eaves, and scratched myself because I was covered with the thing called prickly-heat. Tietjens came out with me and put her head in my lap and was very sorrowful; so I gave her biscuits when tea was ready, and I took tea in the back verandah on account of the little coolness found there. The rooms of the house were dark behind me. I could smell Strickland's saddlery and the oil on his guns, and I had no desire to sit among these things. My own servant came to me in the twilight, the muslin of his clothes clinging tightly to his drenched body, and told me that a gentleman had called and wished to see some one. Very much against my will, but only because of the darkness of the rooms, I went into the naked drawing-room, telling my man to bring the lights. There might or might not have been a caller waiting, it seemed to me that I saw a figure by one of the windows, but when the lights came there was nothing save the spikes of the rain without, and the smell of the drinking earth in my nostrils. I explained to my servant that he was no wiser than he ought to be, and went back to the verandah to talk to Tietjens. She had gone out into the wet, and I could hardly coax her back to me; even with biscuits with sugar tops. Strickland came home, dripping wet, just before dinner, and the first thing he said was.

'Has any one called?'

I explained, with apologies, that my servant had summoned me into the drawing-room on a false alarm; or that some loafer had tried to call on Strickland, and thinking better of it had fled after giving his name. Strickland ordered dinner, without comment, and since it was a real dinner with a white tablecloth attached, we sat down.

At nine o'clock Strickland wanted to go to bed, and I was tired too. Tietjens, who had been lying underneath the table, rose up, and swung into the least exposed verandah as soon as her master moved to his own room, which was next to the stately chamber set apart for Tietjens. If a mere wife had wished to sleep out of doors in that pelting rain it would not have mattered; but Tietjens was a dog, and therefore the better animal. I looked at Strickland, expecting to see him flay her with a whip. He smiled queerly, as a man would smile after telling some unpleasant domestic tragedy. 'She has done this ever since I moved in here,' said he. 'Let her go.'

The dog was Strickland's dog, so I said nothing, but I felt all that Strickland felt In being thus made light of. Tietjens encamped outside my bedroom window, and storm after storm came up, thundered on the thatch, and died away. The lightning spattered the sky as a thrown egg spatters a barn-door, but the light was pale blue, not yellow; and, looking through my split bamboo blinds, I could see the great dog standing, not sleeping, in the verandah, the hackles alift on her back and her feet anchored as tensely as the drawn wire-rope of a suspension bridge. In the very short pauses of the thunder I tried to sleep, but it seemed that some one wanted me very urgently. He, whoever he was, was trying to call me by name, but his voice was no more than a husky whisper. The thunder ceased, and Tietjens went into the garden and howled at the low moon. Somebody tried to open my door, walked about and about through the house and stood breathing heavily in the verandahs, and just when I was falling asleep I fancied that I heard a wild hammering and clamouring above my head or on the door.

I ran into Strickland's room and asked him whether he was ill, and had been calling for me. He was lying on his bed half dressed, a pipe in his mouth. 'I thought you'd come,' he said. 'Have I been walking round the house recently?'

I explained that he had been tramping in the dining-room and the smoking-room and two or three other places, and he laughed and told me to go back to bed. I went back to bed and slept till the morning, but through all my mixed dreams I was sure I was doing some one an injustice in not attending to his wants. What those wants were I could not tell; but a fluttering, whispering, bolt-fumbling, lurking, loitering Someone was reproaching me for my slackness, and, half awake, I heard the howling of Tietjens in the garden and the threshing of the rain.

I lived in that house for two days. Strickland went to his office daily, leaving me alone for eight or ten hours with Tietjens for my only companion. As long as the full light lasted I was comfortable, and so was Tietjens; but in the twilight she and I moved into the back verandah and cuddled each other for company. We were alone in the house, but none the less it was much too fully occupied by a tenant with whom I did not wish to interfere. I never saw him, but I could see the curtains between the rooms quivering where he had just passed through; I could hear the chairs creaking as the bamboos sprung under a weight that had just quitted them; and I could feel when I went to get a book from the dining-room that somebody was waiting in the shadows of the front verandah till I should have gone away. Tietjens made the twilight more interesting by glaring into the darkened rooms with every hair erect, and following the motions of something that I could not see. She never entered the rooms, but her eyes moved interestedly: that was quite sufficient. Only when my servant came to trim the lamps and make all light and habitable she would come in with me and spend her time sitting on her haunches, watching an invisible extra man as he moved about behind my shoulder. Dogs are cheerful companions.

I explained to Strickland, gently as might be, that I would go over to the Club and find for myself quarters there. I admired his hospitality, was pleased with his guns and rods, but I did not much care for his house and its atmosphere. He heard me out to the end, and then smiled very wearily, but without contempt, for he is a man who understands things. 'Stay on,' he said, 'and see what this thing means. All you have talked about I have known since I took the bungalow. Stay on and wait. Tietjens has left me. Are you going too?'

I had seen him through one little affair, connected with a heathen idol, that had brought me to the doors of a lunatic asylum, and I had no desire to help him through further experiences. He was a man to whom unpleasantnesses arrived as do dinners to ordinary people.

Therefore I explained more clearly than ever that I liked him immensely, and would be happy to see him in the daytime; but that I did not care to sleep under his roof. This was after dinner, when Tietjens had gone out to lie in the verandah.

"Pon my soul, I don't wonder,' said Strickland, with his eyes on the ceiling-cloth. 'Look at that!'

The tails of two brown snakes were hanging between the cloth and the cornice of the wall. They threw long shadows in the lamplight.

'If you are afraid of snakes of course' said Strickland.

I hate and fear snakes, because if you look into the eyes of any snake you will see that it knows all and more of the mystery of man's fall, and that it feels all the contempt that the Devil felt when Adam was evicted from Eden. Besides which its bite is generally fatal, and it twists up trouser legs.

'You ought to get your thatch overhauled,' I said.

'Give me a mahseer-rod, and we'll poke 'em down.'

'They'll hide among the roof-beams,' said Strickland. 'I can't stand snakes overhead. I'm going up into the roof. If I shake 'em down, stand by with a cleaning-rod and break their backs.'

I was not anxious to assist Strickland in his work, but I took the cleaning-rod and waited in the dining-room, while Strickland brought a gardener's ladder from the verandah, and set it against the side of the room.

The snake-tails drew themselves up and disappeared. We could hear the dry rushing scuttle of long bodies running over the baggy ceiling-cloth. Strickland took a lamp with him, while I tried to make clear to him the danger of hunting roof-snakes between a ceiling-cloth and a thatch, apart from the deterioration of property caused by ripping out ceiling- cloths.

'Nonsense!' said Strickland. 'They're sure to hide near the walls by the cloth. The bricks are too cold for 'em, and the heat of the room is just what they like.' He put his hand to the corner of the stuff and ripped it from the cornice. It gave with a great sound of tearing, and Strickland put his head through the opening into the dark of the angle of the roof-beams. I set my teeth and lifted the rod, for I had not the least knowledge of what might descend.

'H'm!' said Strickland, and his voice rolled and rumbled in the roof. 'There's room for another set of rooms up here, and, by Jove, some one is occupying 'em!'

'Snakes?' I said from below.

'No. It's a buffalo. Hand me up the two last joints of a mahseer-rod, and I'll prod it. It's lying on the main roof-beam.'

I handed up the rod.

'What a nest for owls and serpents! No wonder the snakes live here,' said Strickland, climbing farther into the roof. I could see his elbow thrusting with the rod. 'Come out of that, whoever you are! Heads below there! It's falling.'

I saw the ceiling-cloth nearly in the centre of the room bag with a shape that was pressing it downwards and downwards towards the lighted lamp on the table. I snatched the lamp out of danger and stood back. Then the cloth ripped out from the walls, tore, split, swayed, and shot down upon the table something that I dared not look at, till Strickland had slid down the ladder and was standing by my side.

He did not say much, being a man of few words; but he picked up the loose end of the tablecloth and threw it over the remnants on the table.

'It strikes me,' said he, putting down the lamp, 'our friend Imray has come back. Oh! you would, would you?'

There was a movement under the cloth, and a little snake wriggled out, to be back-broken by the butt of the mahseer-rod. I was sufficiently sick to make no remarks worth recording.

Strickland meditated, and helped himself to drinks. The arrangement under the cloth made no more signs of life.

'Is it Imray?' I said.

Strickland turned back the cloth for a moment, and looked.

'It is Imray,' he said; 'and his throat is cut from ear to ear.'

Then we spoke, both together and to ourselves: 'That's why he whispered about the house.'

Tietjens, in the garden, began to bay furiously. A little later her great nose heaved open the dining-room door.

She sniffed and was still. The tattered ceiling-cloth hung down almost to the level of the table, and there was hardly room to move away from the discovery.

Tietjens came in and sat down; her teeth bared under her lip and her forepaws planted. She looked at Strickland.

'It's a bad business, old lady,' said he. 'Men don't climb up into the roofs of their bungalows to die, and they don't fasten up the ceiling cloth behind 'em. Let's think it out.'

'Let's think it out somewhere else,' I said.

'Excellent idea! Turn the lamps out. We'll get into my room.'

I did not turn the lamps out. I went into Strickland's room first, and allowed him to make the darkness. Then he followed me, and we lit tobacco and thought. Strickland thought. I smoked furiously, because I was afraid.

'Imray is back,' said Strickland. 'The question is, who killed Imray? Don't talk, I've a notion of my own. When I took this bungalow I took over most of Imray's servants. Imray was guileless and inoffensive, wasn't he?'

I agreed; though the heap under the cloth had looked neither one thing nor the other.

'If I call in all the servants they will stand fast in a crowd and lie like Aryans. What do you suggest?'

'Call 'em in one by one,' I said.

'They'll run away and give the news to all their fellows,' said Strickland. 'We must segregate 'em. Do you suppose your servant knows anything about it?'

'He may, for aught I know; but I don't think it's likely. He has only been here two or three days,' I answered. 'What's your notion?'

'I can't quite tell. How the dickens did the man get the wrong side of the ceiling-cloth?'

There was a heavy coughing outside Strickland's bedroom door. This showed that Bahadur Khan, his body-servant, had waked from sleep and wished to put Strickland to bed.

'Come in,' said Strickland. 'It's a very warm night, isn't it?'

Bahadur Khan, a great, green-turbaned, six-foot Mahomedan, said that it was a very warm night; but that there was more rain pending, which, by his Honour's favour, would bring relief to the country.

'It will be so, if God pleases,' said Strickland, tugging off his boots. 'It is in my mind, Bahadur Khan, that I have worked thee remorselessly for many days, ever since that time when thou first earnest into my service. What time was that?'

'Has the Heaven-born forgotten? It was when Imray Sahib went secretly to Europe without warning given; and I-even I-came into the honoured service of the protector of the poor.'

'And Imray Sahib went to Europe?'

'It is so said among those who were his servants.'

'And thou wilt take service with him when he returns?'

'Assuredly, Sahib. He was a good master, and cherished his dependants.'

'That is true. I am very tired, but I go buck-shooting to-morrow. Give me the little sharp rifle that I use for black-buck; it is in the case yonder.'

The man stooped over the case; handed barrels, stock, and fore-end to Strickland, who fitted all together, yawning dolefully. Then he reached down to the gun-case, took a solid-drawn cartridge, and slipped it into the breech of the '360 Express.

'And Imray Sahib has gone to Europe secretly! That is very strange, Bahadur Khan, is it not?'

'What do I know of the ways of the white man. Heaven-born?'

'Very little, truly. But thou shalt know more anon. It has reached me that Imray Sahib has returned from his so long journeyings, and that even now he lies in the next room, waiting his servant.'

'Sahib!'

The lamplight slid along the barrels of the rifle as they levelled themselves at Bahadur Khan's broad breast.

'Go and look!'said Strickland. 'Take a lamp. Thy master is tired, and he waits thee. Go!'

The man picked up a lamp, and went into the dining-room, Strickland following, and almost pushing him with the muzzle of the rifle. He looked for a moment at the black depths behind the ceiling-cloth; at the writhing snake under foot; and last, a gray glaze settling on his face, at the thing under the tablecloth.

'Hast thou seen?' said Strickland after a pause.

'I have seen. I am clay in the white man's hands. What does the Presence do?'

'Hang thee within the month. What else?'

'For killing him? Nay, Sahib, consider. Walking among us, his servants, he cast his eyes upon my child, who was four years old. Him he bewitched, and in ten days he died of the fever, my child!'

'What said Imray Sahib?'

'He said he was a handsome child, and patted him on the head; wherefore my child died. Wherefore I killed Imray Sahib in the twilight, when he had come back from office, and was sleeping. Wherefore I dragged him up into the roof-beams and made all fast behind him. The Heaven-born knows all things. I am the servant of the Heaven-born.'

Strickland looked at me above the rifle, and said, in the vernacular, 'Thou art witness to this saying? He has killed.'

Bahadur Khan stood ashen gray in the light of the one lamp. The need for justification came upon him very swiftly. 'I am trapped,' he said, 'but the offence was that man's. He cast an evil eye upon my child, and I killed and hid him. Only such as are served by devils,' he glared at Tietjens, couched stolidly before him, 'only such could know what I did.'

'It was clever. But thou shouldst have lashed him to the beam with a rope. Now, thou thyself wilt hang by a rope. Orderly!'

A drowsy policeman answered Strickland's call. He was followed by another, and Tietjens sat wondrous still.

'Take him to the police-station,' said Strickland. 'There is a case toward.'

'Do I hang, then?' said Bahadur Khan, making no attempt to escape, and keeping his eyes on the ground.

'If the sun shines or the water runs-yes!' said Strickland.

Bahadur Khan stepped back one long pace, quivered, and stood still. The two policemen waited further orders.

'Go!'said Strickland.

'Nay; but I go very swiftly,' said Bahadur Khan. 'Look! I am even now a dead man.'

He lifted his foot, and to the little toe there clung the head of the half-killed snake, firm fixed in the agony of death.

'I come of land-holding stock,' said Bahadur Khan, rocking where he stood. 'It were a disgrace to me to go to the public scaffold: therefore I take this way. Be it remembered that the Sahib's shirts are correctly enumerated, and that there is an extra piece of soap in his washbasin. My child was bewitched, and I slew the wizard. Why should you seek to slay me with the rope? My honour is saved, and-and-I die.'

At the end of an hour he died, as they die who are bitten by the little brown karait, and the policemen bore him and the thing under the tablecloth to their appointed places. All were needed to make clear the disappearance of Imray.

'This,' said Strickland, very calmly, as he climbed into bed, 'is called the nineteenth century. Did you hear what that man said?'

'I heard,' I answered. 'Imray made a mistake.'

'Simply and solely through not knowing the nature of the Oriental, and the coincidence of a little seasonal fever. Bahadur Khan had been with him for four years.'

I shuddered. My own servant had been with me for exactly that length of time. When I went over to my own room I found my man waiting, impassive as the copper head on a penny, to pull off my boots.

'What has befallen Bahadur Khan?' said I.

'He was bitten by a snake and died. The rest the Sahib knows,' was the answer.

'And how much of this matter hast thou known?'

'As much as might be gathered from One coming in in the twilight to seek satisfaction. Gently, Sahib. Let me pull off those boots.'

I had just settled to the sleep of exhaustion when I heard Strickland shouting from his side of the house

'Tietjens has come back to her place!'

And so she had. The great deerhound was couched statelily on her own bedstead on her own blanket, while, in the next room, the idle, empty, ceiling-cloth waggled as it trailed on the table.

The Eye Of Apollo by GK Chesterton

That singular smoky sparkle, at once a confusion and a transparency, which is the strange secret of the Thames, was changing more and more from its grey to its glittering extreme as the sun climbed to the zenith over Westminster, and two men crossed Westminster Bridge. One man was very tall and the other very short; they might even have been fantastically compared to the arrogant clock-tower of Parliament and the humbler humped shoulders of the Abbey, for the short man was in clerical dress. The official description of the tall man was M. Hercule Flambeau, private detective, and he was going to his new offices in a new pile of flats facing the Abbey entrance. The official description of the short man was the Reverend J. Brown, attached to St. Francis Xavier's Church, Camberwell, and he was coming from a Camberwell deathbed to see the new offices of his friend.

The building was American in its sky-scraping altitude, and American also in the oiled elaboration of its machinery of telephones and lifts. But it was barely finished and still understaffed; only three tenants had moved in; the office just above Flambeau was occupied, as also was the office just below him; the two floors above that and the three floors below were entirely bare. But the first glance at the new tower of flats caught something much more arresting. Save for a few relics of scaffolding, the one glaring object was erected outside the office just above Flambeau's. It was an enormous gilt effigy of the human eye, surrounded with rays of gold, and taking up as much room as two or three of the office windows.

"What on earth is that?" asked Father Brown, and stood still. "Oh, a new religion," said Flambeau, laughing; "one of those new religions that forgive your sins by saying you never had any. Rather like Christian Science, I should think. The fact is that a fellow calling himself Kalon (I don't know what his name is, except that it can't be that) has taken the flat just above me. I have two lady typewriters underneath me, and this enthusiastic old humbug on top. He calls himself the New Priest of Apollo, and he worships the sun."

"Let him look out," said Father Brown. "The sun was the cruellest of all the gods. But what does that monstrous eye mean?"

"As I understand it, it is a theory of theirs," answered Flambeau, "that a man can endure anything if his mind is quite steady. Their two great symbols are the sun and the open eye; for they say that if a man were really healthy he could stare at the sun."

"If a man were really healthy," said Father Brown, "he would not bother to stare at it."

"Well, that's all I can tell you about the new religion," went on Flambeau carelessly. "It claims, of course, that it can cure all physical diseases."

"Can it cure the one spiritual disease?" asked Father Brown, with a serious curiosity.

"And what is the one spiritual disease?" asked Flambeau, smiling.

"Oh, thinking one is quite well," said his friend.

Flambeau was more interested in the quiet little office below him than in the flamboyant temple above. He was a lucid Southerner, incapable of conceiving himself as anything but a Catholic or an atheist; and new religions of a bright and pallid sort were not much in his line. But humanity was always in his line, especially when it was good-looking; moreover, the ladies downstairs were characters in their way. The office was kept by two sisters, both slight and dark, one of them tall and striking. She had a dark, eager and aquiline profile, and was one of those women whom one always thinks of in profile, as of the clean-cut edge of some weapon. She seemed to cleave her way through life. She had eyes of startling brilliancy, but it was the brilliancy of steel rather than of diamonds; and her straight, slim figure was a shade too stiff for its grace. Her younger sister was like her shortened shadow, a little greyer, paler, and more insignificant. They both wore a business-like black, with little masculine cuffs and collars. There are thousands of such curt, strenuous ladies in the offices of London, but the interest of these lay rather in their real than their apparent position.

For Pauline Stacey, the elder, was actually the heiress of a crest and half a county, as well as great wealth; she had been brought up in castles and gardens, before a frigid fierceness (peculiar to the modern woman) had driven her to what she considered a harsher and a higher existence. She had not, indeed, surrendered her money; in that there would have been a romantic or monkish abandon quite alien to her masterful utilitarianism. She held her wealth, she would say, for use upon practical social objects. Part of it she had put into her business, the nucleus of a model typewriting emporium; part of it was distributed in various leagues and causes for the advancement of such work among women. How far Joan, her sister and partner, shared this slightly prosaic idealism no one could be very sure. But she followed her leader with a dog-like affection which was somehow more attractive, with its touch of tragedy, than the hard, high spirits of the elder. For Pauline Stacey had nothing to say to tragedy; she was understood to deny its existence.

Her rigid rapidity and cold impatience had amused Flambeau very much on the first occasion of his entering the flats. He had lingered outside the lift in the entrance hall waiting for the lift-boy, who generally conducts strangers to the various floors. But this bright-eyed falcon of a girl had openly refused to endure such official delay. She said sharply that she knew all about the lift, and was not dependent on boys or men either. Though her flat was only three floors above, she managed in the few seconds of ascent to give Flambeau a great many of her fundamental views in an off-hand manner; they were to the general effect that she was a modern working woman and loved modern working machinery. Her bright black eyes blazed with abstract anger against those who rebuke mechanic science and ask for the return of romance. Everyone, she said, ought to be able to manage machines, just as she could manage the lift. She seemed almost to resent the fact of Flambeau opening the lift-door for her; and that gentleman went up to his own apartments smiling with somewhat mingled feelings at the memory of such spit-fire self-dependence.

She certainly had a temper, of a snappy, practical sort; the gestures of her thin, elegant hands were abrupt or even destructive.

Once Flambeau entered her office on some typewriting business, and found she had just flung a pair of spectacles belonging to her sister into the middle of the floor and stamped on them. She was already in the rapids of an ethical tirade about the "sickly medical notions" and the morbid admission of weakness implied in such an apparatus. She dared her sister to bring such artificial, unhealthy rubbish into the place again. She asked if she was expected to wear wooden legs or false hair or glass eyes; and as she spoke her eyes sparkled like the terrible crystal.

Flambeau, quite bewildered with this fanaticism, could not refrain from asking Miss Pauline (with direct French logic) why a pair of spectacles was a more morbid sign of weakness than a lift, and why, if science might help us in the one effort, it might not help us in the other.

"That is so different," said Pauline Stacey, loftily. "Batteries and motors and all those things are marks of the force of man, yes, Mr. Flambeau, and the force of woman, too! We shall take our turn at these great engines that devour distance and defy time. That is high and splendid, that is really science. But these nasty props and plasters the doctors sell, why, they are just badges of poltroonery. Doctors stick on legs and arms as if we were born cripples and sick slaves. But I was free-born, Mr. Flambeau! People only think they need these things because they have been trained in fear instead of being trained in power and courage, just as the silly nurses tell children not to stare at the sun, and so they can't do it without blinking. But why among the stars should there be one star I may not see? The sun is not my master, and I will open my eyes and stare at him whenever I choose."

"Your eyes," said Flambeau, with a foreign bow, "will dazzle the sun." He took pleasure in complimenting this strange stiff beauty, partly because it threw her a little off her balance. But as he went upstairs to his floor he drew a deep breath and whistled, saying to himself: "So she has got into the hands of that conjurer upstairs with his golden eye." For, little as he knew or cared about the new religion of Kalon, he had heard of his special notion about sun-gazing.

He soon discovered that the spiritual bond between the floors above and below him was close and increasing. The man who called himself Kalon was a magnificent creature, worthy, in a physical sense, to be the pontiff of Apollo. He was nearly as tall even as Flambeau, and very much better looking, with a golden beard, strong blue eyes, and a mane flung back like a lion's. In structure he was the blonde beast of Nietzsche, but all this animal beauty was heightened, brightened and softened by genuine intellect and spirituality. If he looked like one of the great Saxon kings, he looked like one of the kings that were also saints. And this despite the cockney incongruity of his surroundings; the fact that he had an office half-way up a building in Victoria Street; that the clerk (a commonplace youth in cuffs and collars) sat in the outer room, between him and the corridor; that his name was on a brass plate, and the gilt emblem of his creed hung above his street, like the advertisement of an oculist. All this vulgarity could not take away from the man called Kalon the vivid oppression and inspiration that came from his soul and body. When all was said, a man in the presence of this quack did feel in the presence of a great man. Even in the loose jacket-suit of linen that he wore as a workshop dress in his office he was a fascinating and formidable figure; and when robed in the white vestments and crowned with the golden circlet, in which he daily saluted the sun, he really looked so splendid that the laughter of the street people sometimes died suddenly on their lips. For three times in the day the new sun-worshipper went out on his little balcony, in the face of all Westminster, to say some litany to his shining lord: once at daybreak, once at sunset, and once at the shock of noon. And it was while the shock of noon still shook faintly from the towers of Parliament and parish church that Father Brown, the friend of Flambeau, first looked up and saw the white priest of Apollo.

Flambeau had seen quite enough of these daily salutations of Phoebus, and plunged into the porch of the tall building without even looking for his clerical friend to follow. But Father Brown, whether from a professional interest in ritual or a strong individual interest in tomfoolery, stopped and stared up at the balcony of the sun-worshipper, just as he might have stopped and stared up at a Punch and Judy. Kalon the Prophet was already erect, with argent garments and uplifted hands, and the sound of his strangely penetrating voice could be heard all the way down the busy street uttering his solar litany. He was already in the middle of it; his eyes were fixed upon the flaming disc. It is doubtful if he saw anything or anyone on this earth; it is substantially certain that he did not see a stunted, round-faced priest who, in the crowd below, looked up at him with blinking eyes. That was perhaps the most startling difference between even these two far divided men. Father Brown could not look at anything without blinking; but the priest of Apollo could look on the blaze at noon without a quiver of the eyelid.

"O sun," cried the prophet, "O star that art too great to be allowed among the stars! O fountain that flowest quietly in that secret spot that is called space. White Father of all white unwearied things, white flames and white flowers and white peaks. Father, who art more innocent than all thy most innocent and quiet children; primal purity, into the peace of which"

A rush and crash like the reversed rush of a rocket was cloven with a strident and incessant yelling. Five people rushed into the gate of the mansions as three people rushed out, and for an instant they all deafened each other. The sense of some utterly abrupt horror seemed for a moment to fill half the street with bad news, bad news that was all the worse because no one knew what it was. Two figures remained still after the crash of commotion: the fair priest of Apollo on the balcony above, and the ugly priest of Christ below him.

At last the tall figure and titanic energy of Flambeau appeared in the doorway of the mansions and dominated the little mob. Talking at the top of his voice like a fog-horn, he told somebody or anybody to go for a surgeon; and as he turned back into the dark and thronged entrance his friend Father Brown dipped in insignificantly after him. Even as he ducked and dived through the crowd he could still hear the magnificent melody and monotony of the solar priest still calling on the happy god who is the friend of fountains and flowers.

Father Brown found Flambeau and some six other people standing round the enclosed space into which the lift commonly descended. But the lift had not descended. Something else had descended; something that ought to have come by a lift.

For the last four minutes Flambeau had looked down on it; had seen the brained and bleeding figure of that beautiful woman who denied the existence of tragedy. He had never had the slightest doubt that it was Pauline Stacey; and, though he had sent for a doctor, he had not the slightest doubt that she was dead.

He could not remember for certain whether he had liked her or disliked her; there was so much both to like and dislike. But she had been a person to him, and the unbearable pathos of details and habit stabbed him with all the small daggers of bereavement. He remembered her pretty face and priggish speeches with a sudden secret vividness which is all the bitterness of death. In an instant like a bolt from the blue, like a thunderbolt from nowhere, that beautiful and defiant body had been dashed down the open well of the lift to death at the bottom. Was it suicide? With so insolent an optimist it seemed impossible. Was it murder? But who was there in those hardly inhabited flats to murder anybody? In a rush of raucous words, which he meant to be strong and suddenly found weak, he asked where was that fellow Kalon. A voice, habitually heavy, quiet and full, assured him that Kalon for the last fifteen minutes had been away up on his balcony worshipping his god. When Flambeau heard the voice, and felt the hand of Father Brown, he turned his swarthy face and said abruptly:

"Then, if he has been up there all the time, who can have done it?"

"Perhaps," said the other, "we might go upstairs and find out. We have half an hour before the police will move."

Leaving the body of the slain heiress in charge of the surgeons, Flambeau dashed up the stairs to the typewriting office, found it utterly empty, and then dashed up to his own. Having entered that, he abruptly returned with a new and white face to his friend.

"Her sister," he said, with an unpleasant seriousness, "her sister seems to have gone out for a walk."

Father Brown nodded. "Or, she may have gone up to the office of that sun man," he said. "If I were you I should just verify that, and then let us all talk it over in your office. No," he added suddenly, as if remembering something, "shall I ever get over that stupidity of mine? Of course, in their office downstairs."

Flambeau stared; but he followed the little father downstairs to the empty flat of the Staceys, where that impenetrable pastor took a large red-leather chair in the very entrance, from which he could see the stairs and landings, and waited. He did not wait very long. In about four minutes three figures descended the stairs, alike only in their solemnity. The first was Joan Stacey, the sister of the dead woman, evidently she had been upstairs in the temporary temple of Apollo; the second was the priest of Apollo himself, his litany finished, sweeping down the empty stairs in utter magnificence, something in his white robes, beard and parted hair had the look of Dore's Christ leaving the Pretorium; the third was Flambeau, black browed and somewhat bewildered.

Miss Joan Stacey, dark, with a drawn face and hair prematurely touched with grey, walked straight to her own desk and set out her papers with a practical flap. The mere action rallied everyone else to sanity. If Miss Joan Stacey was a criminal, she was a cool one. Father Brown regarded her for some time with an odd little smile, and then, without taking his eyes off her, addressed himself to somebody else.

"Prophet," he said, presumably addressing Kalon, "I wish you would tell me a lot about your religion."

"I shall be proud to do it," said Kalon, inclining his still crowned head, "but I am not sure that I understand."

"Why, it's like this," said Father Brown, in his frankly doubtful way: "We are taught that if a man has really bad first principles, that must be partly his fault. But, for all that, we can make some difference between a man who insults his quite clear conscience and a man with a conscience more or less clouded with sophistries. Now, do you really think that murder is wrong at all?"

"Is this an accusation?" asked Kalon very quietly.

"No," answered Brown, equally gently, "it is the speech for the defence."

In the long and startled stillness of the room the prophet of Apollo slowly rose; and really it was like the rising of the sun. He filled that room with his light and life in such a manner that a man felt he could as easily have filled Salisbury Plain. His robed form seemed to hang the whole room with classic draperies; his epic gesture seemed to extend it into grander perspectives, till the little black figure of the modern cleric seemed to be a fault and an intrusion, a round, black blot upon some splendour of Hellas.

"We meet at last, Caiaphas," said the prophet. "Your church and mine are the only realities on this earth. I adore the sun, and you the darkening of the sun; you are the priest of the dying and I of the living God. Your present work of suspicion and slander is worthy of your coat and creed. All your church is but a black police; you are only spies and detectives seeking to tear from men confessions of guilt, whether by treachery or torture. You would convict men of crime, I would convict them of innocence. You would convince them of sin, I would convince them of virtue.

"Reader of the books of evil, one more word before I blow away your baseless nightmares for ever. Not even faintly could you understand how little I care whether you can convict me or no. The things you call disgrace and horrible hanging are to me no more than an ogre in a child's toy-book to a man once grown up. You said you were offering the speech for the defence. I care so little for the cloudland of this life that I will offer you the speech for the prosecution. There is but one thing that can be said against me in this matter, and I will say it myself. The woman that is dead was my love and my bride; not after such manner as your tin chapels call lawful, but by a law purer and sterner than you will ever understand. She and I walked another world from yours, and trod palaces of crystal while you were plodding through tunnels and corridors of brick. Well, I know that policemen, theological and otherwise, always fancy that where there has been love there must soon be hatred; so there you have the first point made for the prosecution. But the second point is stronger; I do not grudge it you. Not only is it true that Pauline loved me, but it is also true that this very morning, before she died, she wrote at that table a will leaving me and my new church half a million. Come, where are the handcuffs? Do you suppose I care what foolish things you do with me? Penal servitude will only be like waiting for her at a wayside station. The gallows will only be going to her in a headlong car."

He spoke with the brain-shaking authority of an orator, and Flambeau and Joan Stacey stared at him in amazed admiration. Father Brown's face seemed to express nothing but extreme distress; he looked at the ground with one wrinkle of pain across his forehead. The prophet of the sun leaned easily against the mantelpiece and resumed:

"In a few words I have put before you the whole case against me, the only possible case against me. In fewer words still I will blow it to pieces, so that not a trace of it remains. As to whether I have committed this crime, the truth is in one sentence: I could not have committed this crime. Pauline Stacey fell from this floor to the ground at five minutes past twelve. A hundred people will go into the witness-box and say that I was standing out upon the balcony of my own rooms above from just before the stroke of noon to a quarter-past, the usual period of my public prayers. My clerk (a respectable youth from Clapham, with no sort of connection with me) will swear that he sat in my outer office all the morning, and that no communication passed through. He will swear that I arrived a full ten minutes before the hour, fifteen minutes before any whisper of the accident, and that I did not leave the office or the balcony all that time. No one ever had so complete an alibi; I could subpoena half Westminster. I think you had better put the handcuffs away again. The case is at an end.

"But last of all, that no breath of this idiotic suspicion remain in the air, I will tell you all you want to know. I believe I do know how my unhappy friend came by her death. You can, if you choose, blame me for it, or my faith and philosophy at least; but you certainly cannot lock me up. It is well known to all students of the higher truths that certain adepts and illuminati have in history attained the power of levitation, that is, of being self-sustained upon the empty air. It is but a part of that general conquest of matter which is the main element in our occult wisdom. Poor Pauline was of an impulsive and ambitious temper. I think, to tell the truth, she thought herself somewhat deeper in the mysteries than she was; and she has often said to me, as we went down in the lift together, that if one's will were strong enough, one could float down as harmlessly as a feather. I solemnly believe that in some ecstasy of noble thoughts she attempted the miracle. Her will, or faith, must have failed her at the crucial instant, and the lower law of matter had its horrible revenge. There is the whole story, gentlemen, very sad and, as you think, very presumptuous and wicked, but certainly not criminal or in any way connected with me. In the short-hand of the police-courts, you had better call it suicide. I shall always call it heroic failure for the advance of science and the slow scaling of heaven."

It was the first time Flambeau had ever seen Father Brown vanquished. He still sat looking at the ground, with a painful and corrugated brow, as if in shame. It was impossible to avoid the feeling which the prophet's winged words had fanned, that here was a sullen, professional suspecter of men overwhelmed by a prouder and purer spirit of natural liberty and health. At last he said, blinking as if in bodily distress: "Well, if that is so, sir, you need do no more than take the testamentary paper you spoke of and go. I wonder where the poor lady left it."

"It will be over there on her desk by the door, I think," said Kalon, with that massive innocence of manner that seemed to acquit him wholly. "She told me specially she would write it this morning, and I actually saw her writing as I went up in the lift to my own room."

"Was her door open then?" asked the priest, with his eye on the corner of the matting.

"Yes," said Kalon calmly.

"Ah! it has been open ever since," said the other, and resumed his silent study of the mat.

"There is a paper over here," said the grim Miss Joan, in a somewhat singular voice. She had passed over to her sister's desk by the doorway, and was holding a sheet of blue foolscap in her hand. There was a sour smile on her face that seemed unfit for such a scene or occasion, and Flambeau looked at her with a darkening brow.

Kalon the prophet stood away from the paper with that loyal unconsciousness that had carried him through. But Flambeau took it out of the lady's hand, and read it with the utmost amazement. It did, indeed, begin in the formal manner of a will, but after the words "I give and bequeath all of which I die possessed" the writing abruptly stopped with a set of scratches, and there was no trace of the name of any legatee. Flambeau, in wonder, handed this truncated testament to his clerical friend, who glanced at it and silently gave it to the priest of the sun.

An instant afterwards that pontiff, in his splendid sweeping draperies, had crossed the room in two great strides, and was towering over Joan Stacey, his blue eyes standing from his head.

"What monkey tricks have you been playing here?" he cried. "That's not all Pauline wrote."

They were startled to hear him speak in quite a new voice, with a Yankee shrillness in it; all his grandeur and good English had fallen from him like a cloak.

"That is the only thing on her desk," said Joan, and confronted him steadily with the same smile of evil favour.

Of a sudden the man broke out into blasphemies and cataracts of incredulous words. There was something shocking about the dropping of his mask; it was like a man's real face falling off.

"See here!" he cried in broad American, when he was breathless with cursing, "I may be an adventurer, but I guess you're a murderess. Yes, gentlemen, here's your death explained, and without any levitation. The poor girl is writing a will in my favour; her cursed sister comes in, struggles for the pen, drags her to the well, and throws her down before she can finish it. Sakes! I reckon we want the handcuffs after all."

"As you have truly remarked," replied Joan, with ugly calm, "your clerk is a very respectable young man, who knows the nature of an oath; and he will swear in any court that I was up in your office arranging some typewriting work for five minutes before and five minutes after my sister fell. Mr. Flambeau will tell you that he found me there."

There was a silence.

"Why, then," cried Flambeau, "Pauline was alone when she fell, and it was suicide!"

"She was alone when she fell," said Father Brown, "but it was not suicide."

"Then how did she die?" asked Flambeau impatiently.

"She was murdered."

"But she was alone," objected the detective.

"She was murdered when she was all alone," answered the priest.

All the rest stared at him, but he remained sitting in the same old dejected attitude, with a wrinkle in his round forehead and an appearance of impersonal shame and sorrow; his voice was colourless and sad.

"What I want to know," cried Kalon, with an oath, "is when the police are coming for this bloody and wicked sister. She's killed her flesh and blood; she's robbed me of half a million that was just as sacredly mine as"

"Come, come, prophet," interrupted Flambeau, with a kind of sneer; "remember that all this world is a cloudland."

The hierophant of the sun-god made an effort to climb back on his pedestal. "It is not the mere money," he cried, "though that would equip the cause throughout the world. It is also my beloved one's wishes. To Pauline all this was holy. In Pauline's eyes"

Father Brown suddenly sprang erect, so that his chair fell over flat behind him. He was deathly pale, yet he seemed fired with a hope; his eyes shone.

"That's it!" he cried in a clear voice. "That's the way to begin. In Pauline's eyes"

The tall prophet retreated before the tiny priest in an almost mad disorder. "What do you mean? How dare you?" he cried repeatedly.

"In Pauline's eyes," repeated the priest, his own shining more and more. "Go on, in God's name, go on. The foulest crime the fiends ever prompted feels lighter after confession; and I implore you to confess. Go on, go on, in Pauline's eyes"

"Let me go, you devil!" thundered Kalon, struggling like a giant in bonds. "Who are you, you cursed spy, to weave your spiders' webs round me, and peep and peer? Let me go."

"Shall I stop him?" asked Flambeau, bounding towards the exit, for Kalon had already thrown the door wide open.

"No; let him pass," said Father Brown, with a strange deep sigh that seemed to come from the depths of the universe. "Let Cain pass by, for he belongs to God."

There was a long-drawn silence in the room when he had left it, which was to Flambeau's fierce wits one long agony of interrogation. Miss Joan Stacey very coolly tidied up the papers on her desk.

"Father," said Flambeau at last, "it is my duty, not my curiosity only, it is my duty to find out, if I can, who committed the crime."

"Which crime?" asked Father Brown.

"The one we are dealing with, of course," replied his impatient friend.

"We are dealing with two crimes," said Brown, "crimes of very different weight, and by very different criminals."

Miss Joan Stacey, having collected and put away her papers, proceeded to lock up her drawer. Father Brown went on, noticing her as little as she noticed him.

"The two crimes," he observed, "were committed against the same weakness of the same person, in a struggle for her money. The author of the larger crime found himself thwarted by the smaller crime; the author of the smaller crime got the money."

"Oh, don't go on like a lecturer," groaned Flambeau; "put it in a few words."

"I can put it in one word," answered his friend.

Miss Joan Stacey skewered her business-like black hat on to her head with a business-like black frown before a little mirror, and, as the conversation proceeded, took her handbag and umbrella in an unhurried style, and left the room.

"The truth is one word, and a short one," said Father Brown. "Pauline Stacey was blind."

"Blind!" repeated Flambeau, and rose slowly to his whole huge stature.

"She was subject to it by blood," Brown proceeded. "Her sister would have started eyeglasses if Pauline would have let her; but it was her special philosophy or fad that one must not encourage such diseases by yielding to them. She would not admit the cloud; or she tried to dispel it by will. So her eyes got worse and worse with straining; but the worst strain was to come. It came with this precious prophet, or whatever he calls himself, who taught her to stare at the hot sun with the naked eye. It was called accepting Apollo. Oh, if these new pagans would only be old pagans, they would be a little wiser! The old pagans knew that mere naked Nature-worship must have a cruel side. They knew that the eye of Apollo can blast and blind."

There was a pause, and the priest went on in a gentle and even broken voice. "Whether or no that devil deliberately made her blind, there is no doubt that he deliberately killed her through her blindness. The very simplicity of the crime is sickening. You know he and she went up and down in those lifts without official help; you know also how smoothly and silently the lifts slide. Kalon brought the lift to the girl's landing, and saw her, through the open door, writing in her slow, sightless way the will she had promised him. He called out to her cheerily that he had the lift ready for her, and she was to come out when she was ready. Then he pressed a button and shot soundlessly up to his own floor, walked through his own office, out on to his own balcony, and was safely praying before the crowded street when the poor girl, having finished her work, ran gaily out to where lover and lift were to receive her, and stepped"

"Don't!" cried Flambeau.

"He ought to have got half a million by pressing that button," continued the little father, in the colourless voice in which he talked of such horrors. "But that went smash. It went smash because there happened to be another person who also wanted the money, and who also knew the secret about poor Pauline's sight. There was one thing about that will that I think nobody noticed: although it was unfinished and without signature, the other Miss Stacey and some servant of hers had already signed it as witnesses. Joan had signed first, saying Pauline could finish it later, with a typical feminine contempt for legal forms. Therefore, Joan wanted her sister to sign the will without real witnesses. Why? I thought of the blindness, and felt sure she had wanted Pauline to sign in solitude because she had wanted her not to sign at all.

"People like the Staceys always use fountain pens; but this was specially natural to Pauline. By habit and her strong will and memory she could still write almost as well as if she saw; but she could not tell when her pen needed dipping. Therefore, her fountain pens were carefully filled by her sister, all except this fountain pen. This was carefully not filled by her sister; the remains of the ink held out for a few lines and then failed altogether. And the prophet lost five hundred thousand pounds and committed one of the most brutal and brilliant murders in human history for nothing."

Flambeau went to the open door and heard the official police ascending the stairs. He turned and said: "You must have followed everything devilish close to have traced the crime to Kalon in ten minutes."

Father Brown gave a sort of start.

"Oh! to him," he said. "No; I had to follow rather close to find out about Miss Joan and the fountain pen. But I knew Kalon was the criminal before I came into the front door."

"You must be joking!" cried Flambeau.

"I'm quite serious," answered the priest. "I tell you I knew he had done it, even before I knew what he had done."

"But why?"

"These pagan stoics," said Brown reflectively, "always fail by their strength. There came a crash and a scream down the street, and the priest of Apollo did not start or look round. I did not know what it was. But I knew that he was expecting it."

The Adventure Of The Copper Beeches by Arthur Conan Doyle

"To the man who loves art for its own sake," remarked Sherlock Holmes, tossing aside the advertisement sheet of the Daily Telegraph, "it is frequently in its least important and lowliest manifestations that the keenest pleasure is to be derived. It is pleasant to me to observe, Watson, that you have so far grasped this truth that in these little records of our cases which you have been good enough to draw up, and, I am bound to say, occasionally to embellish, you have given prominence not so much to the many causes celebres and sensational trials in which I have figured but rather to those incidents which may have been trivial in themselves, but which have given room for those faculties of deduction and of logical synthesis which I have made my special province."

"And yet," said I, smiling, "I cannot quite hold myself absolved from the charge of sensationalism which has been urged against my records."

"You have erred, perhaps," he observed, taking up a glowing cinder with the tongs and lighting with it the long cherry-wood pipe which was wont to replace his clay when he was in a disputatious rather than a meditative mood "you have erred perhaps in attempting to put color and life into each of your statements instead of confining yourself to the task of placing upon record that severe reasoning from cause to effect which is really the only notable feature about the thing."

"It seems to me that I have done you full justice in the matter," I remarked with some coldness, for I was repelled by the egotism which I had more than once observed to be a strong factor in my friend's singular character.

"No, it is not selfishness or conceit," said he, answering, as was his wont, my thoughts rather than my words. "If I claim full justice for my art, it is because it is an impersonal thing, a thing beyond myself. Crime is common. Logic is rare. Therefore it is upon the logic rather than upon the crime that you should dwell. You have degraded what should have been a course of lectures into a series of tales."

It was a cold morning of the early spring, and we sat after breakfast on either side of a cheery fire in the old room at Baker Street. A thick fog rolled down between the lines of dun-colored houses, and the opposing windows loomed like dark, shapeless blurs through the heavy yellow wreaths. Our gas was lit and shone on the white cloth and glimmer of china and metal, for the table had not been cleared yet. Sherlock Holmes had been silent all the morning, dipping continuously into the advertisement columns of a succession of papers until at last, having apparently given up his search, he had emerged in no very sweet temper to lecture me upon my literary shortcomings.

"At the same time," he remarked after a pause, during which he had sat puffing at his long pipe and gazing down into the fire, "you can hardly be open to a charge of sensationalism, for out of these cases which you have been so kind as to interest yourself in, a fair proportion do not treat of crime, in its legal sense, at all. The small matter in which I endeavored to help the King of Bohemia, the singular experience of Miss Mary Sutherland, the problem connected with the man with the twisted lip, and the incident of the noble bachelor, were all matters which are outside the pale of the law. But in avoiding the sensational, I fear that you may have bordered on the trivial."

"The end may have been so," I answered, "but the methods I hold to have been novel and of interest."

"Pshaw, my dear fellow, what do the public, the great unobservant public, who could hardly tell a weaver by his tooth or a compositor by his left thumb, care about the finer shades of analysis and deduction! But, indeed, if you are trivial. I cannot blame you, for the days of the great cases are past. Man, or at least criminal man, has lost all enterprise and originality. As to my own little practice, it seems to be degenerating into an agency for recovering lost lead pencils and giving advice to young ladies from boarding-schools. I think that I have touched bottom at last, however. This note I had this morning marks my zero-point, I fancy. Read it!" He tossed a crumpled letter across to me.

It was dated from Montague Place upon the preceding evening, and ran thus:

"DEAR MR. HOLMES,

I am very anxious to consult you as to whether I should or should not accept a situation which has been offered to me as governess. I shall call at half-past ten to-morrow if I do not inconvenience you.

"Yours faithfully,

"VIOLET HUNTER."

"Do you know the young lady?" I asked.

"Not I."

"It is half-past ten now."

"Yes, and I have no doubt that is her ring."

"It may turn out to be of more interest than you think. You remember that the affair of the blue carbuncle, which appeared to be a mere whim at first, developed into a serious investigation. It may be so in this case, also."

"Well, let us hope so. But our doubts will very soon be solved, for here, unless I am much mistaken, is the person in question."

As he spoke the door opened and a young lady entered the room. She was plainly but neatly dressed, with a bright, quick face, freckled like a plover's egg, and with the brisk manner of a woman who has had her own way to make in the world.

"You will excuse my troubling you, I am sure," said she, as my companion rose to greet her, "but I have had a very strange experience, and as I have no parents or relations of any sort from whom I could ask advice, I thought that perhaps you would be kind enough to tell me what I should do."

"Pray take a seat, Miss Hunter. I shall be happy to do anything that I can to serve you."

I could see that Holmes was favorably impressed by the manner and speech of his new client. He looked her over in his searching fashion, and then composed himself, with his lids drooping and his finger-tips together, to listen to her story.

"I have been a governess for five years," said she, "in the family of Colonel Spence Munro, but two months ago the colonel received an appointment at Halifax, in Nova Scotia, and took his children over to America with him, so that I found myself without a situation. I advertised, and I answered advertisements, but without success. At last the little money which I had saved began to run short, and I was at my wit's end as to what I should do.

"There is a well-known agency for governesses in the West End called Westaway's, and there I used to call about once a week in order to see whether anything had turned up which might suit me. Westaway was the name of the founder of the business, but it is really managed by Miss Stoper. She sits in her own little office, and the ladies who are seeking employment wait in an anteroom, and are then shown in one by one, when she consults her ledgers and sees whether she has anything which would suit them.

"Well, when I called last week I was shown into the little office as usual, but I found that Miss Stoper was not alone. A prodigiously stout man with a very smiling face and a great heavy chin which rolled down in fold upon fold over his throat sat at her elbow with a pair of glasses on his nose, looking very earnestly at the ladies who entered. As I came in he gave quite a jump in his chair and turned quickly to Miss Stoper.

"'That will do,' said he; 'I could not ask for anything better. Capital! capital!' He seemed quite enthusiastic and rubbed his hands together in the most genial fashion. He was such a comfortable-looking man that it was quite a pleasure to look at him.

"'You are looking for a situation, miss?' he asked.

"'Yes, sir.'

"'As governess?'

"'Yes, sir.'

"'And what salary do you ask?'

"'I had 4 pounds a month in my last place with Colonel Spence Munro.'

"'Oh, tut, tut! Sweating, rank sweating!' he cried, throwing his fat hands out into the air like a man who is in a boiling passion. 'How could anyone offer so pitiful a sum to a lady with such attractions and accomplishments?'

"'My accomplishments, sir, may be less than you imagine,' said I. 'A little French, a little German, music, and drawing'

"'Tut, tut!' he cried. 'This is all quite beside the question. The point is, have you or have you not the bearing and deportment of a lady? There it is in a nutshell. If you have not, you are not fined for the rearing of a child who may some day play a considerable part in the history of the country. But if you have why, then, how could any gentleman ask you to condescend to accept anything under the three figures? Your salary with me, madam, would commence at 100 pounds a year.'

"You may imagine, Mr. Holmes, that to me, destitute as I was, such an offer seemed almost too good to be true. The gentleman, however, seeing perhaps the look of incredulity upon my face, opened a pocket-book and took out a note.

"'It is also my custom,' said he, smiling in the most pleasant fashion until his eyes were just two little shining slits amid the white creases of his face, 'to advance to my young ladies half their salary beforehand, so that they may meet any little expenses of their journey and their wardrobe.'

"It seemed to me that I had never met so fascinating and so thoughtful a man. As I was already in debt to my tradesmen, the advance was a great convenience, and yet there was something unnatural about the whole transaction which made me wish to know a little more before I quite committed myself.

"'May I ask where you live, sir?' said I.

"'Hampshire. Charming rural place. The Copper Beeches, five miles on the far side of Winchester. It is the most lovely country, my dear young lady, and the dearest old country-house.'

"'And my duties, sir? I should be glad to know what they would be.'

"'One child, one dear little romper just six years old. Oh, if you could see him killing cockroaches with a slipper! Smack! smack! smack! Three gone before you could wink!' He leaned back in his chair and laughed his eyes into his head again.

"I was a little startled at the nature of the child's amusement, but the father's laughter made me think that perhaps he was joking.

"'My sole duties, then,' I asked, 'are to take charge of a single child?'

"'No, no, not the sole, not the sole, my dear young lady,' he cried. 'Your duty would be, as I am sure your good sense would suggest, to obey any little commands my wife might give, provided always that they were such commands as a lady might with propriety obey. You see no difficulty, heh?'

"'I should be happy to make myself useful.'

"'Quite so. In dress now, for example. We are faddy people, you know, faddy but kind-hearted. If you were asked to wear any dress which we might give you, you would not object to our little whim. Heh?'

"'No,' said I, considerably astonished at his words.

"'Or to sit here, or sit there, that would not be offensive to you?'

"'Oh, no.'

"'Or to cut your hair quite short before you come to us?'

"I could hardly believe my ears. As you may observe, Mr. Holmes, my hair is somewhat luxuriant, and of a rather peculiar tint of chestnut. It has been considered artistic. I could not dream of sacrificing it in this offhand fashion.

"'I am afraid that that is quite impossible,' said I. He had been watching me eagerly out of his small eyes, and I could see a shadow pass over his face as I spoke.

"'I am afraid that it is quite essential,' said he. 'It is a little fancy of my wife's, and ladies' fancies, you know, madam, ladies' fancies must be consulted. And so you won't cut your hair?'

"'No, sir, I really could not,' I answered firmly.

"'Ah, very well; then that quite settles the matter. It is a pity, because in other respects you would really have done very nicely. In that case, Miss Stoper, I had best inspect a few more of your young ladies.'

"The manageress had sat all this while busy with her papers without a word to either of us, but she glanced at me now with so much annoyance upon her face that I could not help suspecting that she had lost a handsome commission through my refusal.

"'Do you desire your name to be kept upon the books?' she asked.

"'If you please, Miss Stoper.'

"'Well, really, it seems rather useless, since you refuse the most excellent offers in this fashion,' said she sharply. 'You can hardly expect us to exert ourselves to find another such opening for you. Good-day to you, Miss Hunter.' She struck a gong upon the table, and I was shown out by the page.

"Well, Mr. Holmes, when I got back to my lodgings and found little enough in the cupboard, and two or three bills upon the table. I began to ask myself whether I had not done a very foolish thing. After all, if these people had strange fads and expected obedience on the most extraordinary matters, they were at least ready to pay for their eccentricity. Very few governesses in England are getting 100 pounds a year. Besides, what use was my hair to me? Many people are improved by wearing it short and perhaps I should be among the number. Next day I was inclined to think that I had made a mistake, and by the day after I was sure of it. I had almost overcome my pride so far as to go back to the agency and inquire whether the place was still open when I received this letter from the gentleman himself. I have it here and I will read it to you:

"'The Copper Beeches, near Winchester.

"'DEAR MISS HUNTER,

"'Miss Stoper has very kindly given me your address, and I write from here to ask you whether you have reconsidered your decision. My wife is very anxious that you should come, for she has been much attracted by my description of you. We are willing to give 30 pounds a quarter, or 120 pounds a year, so as to recompense you for any little inconvenience which our fads may cause you. They are not very exacting, after all. My wife is fond of a particular shade of electric blue and would like you to wear such a dress indoors in the morning. You need not, however, go to the expense of purchasing one, as we have one belonging to my dear daughter Alice (now in Philadelphia), which would, I should think, fit you very well. Then, as to sitting here or there,or amusing yourself in any manner indicated, that need cause you no inconvenience. As regards your hair, it is no doubt a pity, especially as I could not help remarking its beauty during our short interview, but I am afraid that I must remain firm upon this point, and I only hope that the increased salary may recompense you for the loss. Your duties, as far as the child is concerned, are very light. Now do try to come, and I shall meet you with the dog-cart at Winchester. Let me know your train.

"'Yours faithfully,

"'JEPHRO RUCASTLE.'

"That is the letter which I have just received, Mr. Holmes, and my mind is made up that I will accept it. I thought, however, that before taking the final step I should like to submit the whole matter to your consideration."

"Well, Miss Hunter, if your mind is made up, that settles the question," said Holmes, smiling.

"But you would not advise me to refuse?"

"I confess that it is not the situation which I should like to see a sister of mine apply for."

"What is the meaning of it all, Mr. Holmes?"

"Ah, I have no data. I cannot tell. Perhaps you have yourself formed some opinion?"

"Well, there seems to me to be only one possible solution. Mr. Rucastle seemed to be a very kind, good-natured man. Is it not possible that his wife is a lunatic, that he desires to keep the matter quiet for fear she should be taken to an asylum, and that he humours her fancies in every way in order to prevent an outbreak?"

"That is a possible solution, in fact, as matters stand, it is the most probable one. But in any case it does not seem to be a nice household for a young lady."

"But the money, Mr. Holmes the money!"

"Well, yes, of course the pay is good, too good. That is what makes me uneasy. Why should they give you 120 pounds a year, when they could have their pick for 40 pounds? There must be some strong reason behind."

"I thought that if I told you the circumstances you would understand afterwards if I wanted your help. I should feel so much stronger if I felt that you were at the back of me."

"Oh, you may carry that feeling away with you. I assure you that your little problem promises to be the most interesting which has come my way for some months. There is something distinctly novel about some of the features. If you should find yourself in doubt or in danger"

"Danger! What danger do you foresee?"

Holmes shook his head gravely. "It would cease to be a danger if we could define it," said he. "But at any time, day or night, a telegram would bring me down to your help."

"That is enough." She rose briskly from her chair with the anxiety all swept from her face. "I shall go down to Hampshire quite easy in my mind now. I shall write to Mr. Rucastle at once, sacrifice my poor hair to-night, and start for Winchester to-morrow." With a few grateful words to Holmes she bade us both good-night and bustled off upon her way.

"At least," said I as we heard her quick, firm steps descending the stairs, "she seems to be a young lady who is very well able to take care of herself."

"And she would need to be," said Holmes gravely. "I am much mistaken if we do not hear from her before many days are past."

It was not very long before my friend's prediction was fulfilled. A fortnight went by, during which I frequently found my thoughts turning in her direction and wondering what strange side-alley of human experience this lonely woman had strayed into. The unusual salary, the curious conditions, the light duties, all pointed to something abnormal, though whether a fad or a plot, or whether the man were a philanthropist or a villain, it was quite beyond my powers to determine. As to Holmes, I observed that he sat frequently for half an hour on end, with knitted brows and an abstracted air, but he swept the matter away with a wave of his hand when I mentioned it. "Data! data! data!" he cried impatiently. "I can't make bricks without clay." And yet he would always wind up by muttering that no sister of his should ever have accepted such a situation.

The telegram which we eventually received came late one night just as I was thinking of turning in and Holmes was settling down to one of those all-night chemical researches which he frequently indulged in, when I would leave him stooping over a retort and a test-tube at night and find him in the same position when I came down to breakfast in the morning. He opened the yellow envelope, and then, glancing at the message, threw it across to me.

"Just look up the trains in Bradshaw," said he, and turned back to his chemical studies.

The summons was a brief and urgent one:

"Please be at the Black Swan Hotel at Winchester at midday to-morrow," it said."Do come! I am at my wit's end. HUNTER."

"Will you come with me?" asked Holmes, glancing up.

"I should wish to."

"Just look it up, then."

"There is a train at half-past nine," said I, glancing over my Bradshaw. "It is due at Winchester at 11:30."

"That will do very nicely. Then perhaps I had better postpone my analysis of the acetones, as we may need to be at our best in the morning."

By eleven o'clock the next day we were well upon our way to the old English capital. Holmes had been buried in the morning papers all the way down, but after we had passed the Hampshire border he threw them down and began to admire the scenery. It was an ideal spring day, a light blue sky, flecked with little fleecy white clouds drifting across from west to east. The sun was shining very brightly, and yet there was an exhilarating nip in the air, which set an edge to a man's energy. All over the countryside, away to the rolling hills around Aldershot, the little red and gray roofs of the farm-steadings peeped out from amid the light green of the new foliage.

"Are they not fresh and beautiful?" I cried with all the enthusiasm of a man fresh from the fogs of Baker Street.

But Holmes shook his head gravely.

"Do you know, Watson," said he, "that it is one of the curses of a mind with a turn like mine that I must look at everything with reference to my own special subject. You look at these scattered houses, and you are impressed by their beauty. I look at them, and the only thought which comes to me is a feeling of their isolation and of the impunity with which crime may be committed there."

"Good heavens!" I cried. "Who would associate crime with these dear old homesteads?"

"They always fill me with a certain horror. It is my belief, Watson, founded upon my experience, that the lowest and vilest alleys in London do not present a more dreadful record of sin than does the smiling and beautiful countryside."

"You horrify me!"

"But the reason is very obvious. The pressure of public opinion can do in the town what the law cannot accomplish. There is no lane so vile that the scream of a tortured child, or the thud of a drunkard's blow, does not beget sympathy and indignation among the neighbors, and then the whole machinery of justice is ever so close that a word of complaint can set it going, and there is but a step between the crime and the dock. But look at these lonely houses, each in its own fields, filled for the most part with poor ignorant folk who know little of the law. Think of the deeds of hellish cruelty, the hidden wickedness which may go on, year in, year out, in such places, and none the wiser. Had this lady who appeals to us for help gone to live in Winchester, I should never have had a fear for her. It is the five miles of country which makes the danger. Still, it is clear that she is not personally threatened."

"No. If she can come to Winchester to meet us she can get away."

"Quite so. She has her freedom."

"What CAN be the matter, then? Can you suggest no explanation?"

"I have devised seven separate explanations, each of which would cover the facts as far as we know them. But which of these is correct can only be determined by the fresh information which we shall no doubt find waiting for us. Well, there is the tower of the cathedral, and we shall soon learn all that Miss Hunter has to tell."

The Black Swan is an inn of repute in the High Street, at no distance from the station, and there we found the young lady waiting for us. She had engaged a sitting-room, and our lunch awaited us upon the table.

"I am so delighted that you have come," she said earnestly. "It is so very kind of you both; but indeed I do not know what I should do. Your advice will be altogether invaluable to me."

"Pray tell us what has happened to you."

"I will do so, and I must be quick, for I have promised Mr. Rucastle to be back before three. I got his leave to come into town this morning, though he little knew for what purpose."

"Let us have everything in its due order." Holmes thrust his long thin legs out towards the fire and composed himself to listen.

"In the first place, I may say that I have met, on the whole, with no actual ill-treatment from Mr. and Mrs. Rucastle. It is only fair to them to say that. But I cannot understand them, and I am not easy in my mind about them."

"What can you not understand?"

"Their reasons for their conduct. But you shall have it all just as it occurred. When I came down, Mr. Rucastle met me here and drove me in his dog-cart to the Copper Beeches. It is, as he said, beautifully situated, but it is not beautiful in itself, for it is a large square block of a house, whitewashed, but all stained and streaked with damp and bad weather. There are grounds round it, woods on three sides, and on the fourth a field which slopes down to the Southampton highroad, which curves past about a hundred yards from the front door. This ground in front belongs to the house, but the woods all round are part of Lord Southerton's preserves. A clump of copper beeches immediately in front of the hall door has given its name to the place.

"I was driven over by my employer, who was as amiable as ever, and was introduced by him that evening to his wife and the child. There was no truth, Mr. Holmes, in the conjecture which seemed to us to be probable in your rooms at Baker Street. Mrs. Rucastle is not mad. I found her to be a silent, pale-faced woman, much younger than her husband, not more than thirty, I should think, while he can hardly be less than forty-five. From their conversation I have gathered that they have been married about seven years, that he was a widower, and that his only child by the first wife was the daughter who has gone to Philadelphia. Mr. Rucastle told me in private that the reason why she had left them was that she had an unreasoning aversion to her stepmother. As the daughter could not have been less than twenty, I can quite imagine that her position must have been uncomfortable with her father's young wife.

"Mrs. Rucastle seemed to me to be colorless in mind as well as in feature. She impressed me neither favorably nor the reverse. She was a nonentity. It was easy to see that she was passionately devoted both to her husband and to her little son. Her light gray eyes wandered continually from one to the other, noting every little want and forestalling it if possible. He was kind to her also in his bluff, boisterous fashion, and on the whole they seemed to be a happy couple. And yet she had some secret sorrow, this woman. She would often be lost in deep thought, with the saddest look upon her face. More than once I have surprised her in tears. I have thought sometimes that it was the disposition of her child which weighed upon her mind, for I have never met so utterly spoiled and so ill-natured a little creature. He is small for his age, with a head which is quite disproportionately large. His whole life appears to be spent in an alternation between savage fits of passion and gloomy intervals of sulking. Giving pain to any creature weaker than himself seems to be his one idea of amusement, and he shows quite remarkable talent in planning the capture of mice, little birds, and insects. But I would rather not talk about the creature, Mr. Holmes, and, indeed, he has little to do with my story."

"I am glad of all details," remarked my friend, "whether they seem to you to be relevant or not."

"I shall try not to miss anything of importance. The one unpleasant thing about the house, which struck me at once, was the appearance and conduct of the servants. There are only two, a man and his wife. Toller, for that is his name, is a rough, uncouth man, with grizzled hair and whiskers, and a perpetual smell of drink. Twice since I have been with them he has been quite drunk, and yet Mr. Rucastle seemed to take no notice of it. His wife is a very tall and strong woman with a sour face, as silent as Mrs. Rucastle and much less amiable. They are a most unpleasant couple, but fortunately I spend most of my time in the nursery and my own room, which are next to each other in one corner of the building.

"For two days after my arrival at the Copper Beeches my life was very quiet; on the third, Mrs. Rucastle came down just after breakfast and whispered something to her husband.

"'Oh, yes,' said he, turning to me, 'we are very much obliged to you, Miss Hunter, for falling in with our whims so far as to cut your hair. I assure you that it has not detracted in the tiniest iota from your appearance. We shall now see how the electric-blue dress will become you. You will find it laid out upon the bed in your room, and if you would be so good as to put it on we should both be extremely obliged.'

"The dress which I found waiting for me was of a peculiar shade of blue. It was of excellent material, a sort of beige, but it bore unmistakable signs of having been worn before. It could not have been a better fit if I had been measured for it. Both Mr. and Mrs. Rucastle expressed a delight at the look of it, which seemed quite exaggerated in its vehemence. They were waiting for me in the drawing-room, which is a very large room, stretching along the entire front of the house, with three long windows reaching down to the floor. A chair had been placed close to the central window, with its back turned towards it. In this I was asked to sit, and then Mr. Rucastle, walking up and down on the other side of the room, began to tell me a series of the funniest stories that I have ever listened to. You cannot imagine how comical he was, and I laughed until I was quite weary. Mrs. Rucastle, however, who has evidently no sense of humour, never so much as smiled, but sat with her hands in her lap, and a sad, anxious look upon her face. After an hour or so, Mr. Rucastle suddenly remarked that it was time to commence the duties of the day, and that I might change my dress and go to little Edward in the nursery.

"Two days later this same performance was gone through under exactly similar circumstances. Again I changed my dress, again I sat in the window, and again I laughed very heartily at the funny stories of which my employer had an immense repertoire, and which he told inimitably. Then he handed me a yellow-backed novel, and moving my chair a little sideways, that my own shadow might not fall upon the page, he begged me to read aloud to him. I read for about ten minutes, beginning in the heart of a chapter, and then suddenly, in the middle of a sentence, he ordered me to cease and to change my dress.

"You can easily imagine, Mr. Holmes, how curious I became as to what the meaning of this extraordinary performance could possibly be. They were always very careful, I observed, to turn my face away from the window, so that I became consumed with the desire to see what was going on behind my back. At first it seemed to be impossible, but I soon devised a means. My hand-mirror had been broken, so a happy thought seized me, and I concealed a piece of the glass in my handkerchief. On the next occasion, in the midst of my laughter, I put my handkerchief up to my eyes, and was able with a little management to see all that there was behind me. I confess that I was disappointed. There was nothing. At least that was my first impression. At the second glance, however, I perceived that there was a man standing in the Southampton Road, a small bearded man in a gray suit, who seemed to be looking in my direction. The road is an important highway, and there are usually people there. This man, however, was leaning against the railings which bordered our field and was looking earnestly up. I lowered my handkerchief and glanced at Mrs. Rucastle to find her eyes fixed upon me with a most searching gaze. She said nothing, but I am convinced that she had divined that I had a mirror in my hand and had seen what was behind me. She rose at once.

"'Jephro,' said she, 'there is an impertinent fellow upon the road there who stares up at Miss Hunter.'

"'No friend of yours, Miss Hunter?' he asked.

"'No, I know no one in these parts.'

"'Dear me! How very impertinent! Kindly turn round and motion to him to go away.'

"'Surely it would be better to take no notice.'

"'No, no, we should have him loitering here always. Kindly turn round and wave him away like that.'

"I did as I was told, and at the same instant Mrs. Rucastle drew down the blind. That was a week ago, and from that time I have not sat again in the window, nor have I worn the blue dress, nor seen the man in the road."

"Pray continue," said Holmes. "Your narrative promises to be a most interesting one."

"You will find it rather disconnected, I fear, and there may prove to be little relation between the different incidents of which I speak. On the very first day that I was at the Copper Beeches, Mr. Rucastle took me to a small outhouse which stands near the kitchen door. As we approached it I heard the sharp rattling of a chain, and the sound as of a large animal moving about.

"'Look in here!' said Mr. Rucastle, showing me a slit between two planks. 'Is he not a beauty?'

"I looked through and was conscious of two glowing eyes, and of a vague figure huddled up in the darkness.

"'Don't be frightened,' said my employer, laughing at the start which I had given. 'It's only Carlo, my mastiff. I call him mine, but really old Toller, my groom, is the only man who can do anything with him. We feed him once a day, and not too much then, so that he is always as keen as mustard. Toller lets him loose every night, and God help the trespasser whom he lays his fangs upon. For goodness' sake don't you ever on any pretext set your foot over the threshold at night, for it's as much as your life is worth.'

"The warning was no idle one, for two nights later I happened to look out of my bedroom window about two o'clock in the morning. It was a beautiful moonlight night, and the lawn in front of the house was silvered over and almost as bright as day. I was standing, rapt in the peaceful beauty of the scene, when I was aware that something was moving under the shadow of the copper beeches. As it emerged into the moonshine I saw what it was. It was a giant dog, as large as a calf, tawny tinted, with hanging jowl, black muzzle, and huge projecting bones. It walked slowly across the lawn and vanished into the shadow upon the other side. That dreadful sentinel sent a chill to my heart which I do not think that any burglar could have done.

"And now I have a very strange experience to tell you. I had, as you know, cut off my hair in London, and I had placed it in a great coil at the bottom of my trunk. One evening, after the child was in bed, I began to amuse myself by examining the furniture of my room and by rearranging my own little things. There was an old chest of drawers in the room, the two upper ones empty and open, the lower one locked. I had filled the first two with my linen. and as I had still much to pack away I was naturally annoyed at not having the use of the third drawer. It struck me that it might have been fastened by a mere oversight, so I took out my bunch of keys and tried to open it. The very first key fitted to perfection, and I drew the drawer open. There was only one thing in it, but I am sure that you would never guess what it was. It was my coil of hair.

"I took it up and examined it. It was of the same peculiar tint, and the same thickness. But then the impossibility of the thing obtruded itself upon me. How could my hair have been locked in the drawer? With trembling hands I undid my trunk, turned out the contents, and drew from the bonom my own hair. I laid the two tresses together, and I assure you that they were identical. Was it not extraordinary? Puzzle as I would, I could make nothing at all of what it meant. I returned the strange hair to the drawer, and I said nothing of the matter to the Rucastles as I felt that I had put myself in the wrong by opening a drawer which they had locked.

"I am naturally observant, as you may have remarked, Mr. Holmes, and I soon had a pretty good plan of the whole house in my head. There was one wing, however, which appeared not to be inhabited at all. A door which faced that which led into the quarters of the Tollers opened into this suite, but it was invariably locked. One day, however, as I ascended the stair, I met Mr. Rucastle coming out through this door, his keys in his hand, and a look on his face which made him a very different person to the round, jovial man to whom I was accustomed. His cheeks were red, his brow was all crinkled with anger, and the veins stood out at his temples with passion. He locked the door and hurried past me without a word or a look.

"This aroused my curiosity, so when I went out for a walk in the grounds with my charge, I strolled round to the side from which I could see the windows of this part of the house. There were four of them in a row, three of which were simply dirty, while the fourth was shuttered up. They were evidently all deserted. As I strolled up and down, glancing at them occasionally, Mr. Rucastle came out to me, looking as merry and jovial as ever.

"'Ah!' said he, 'you must not think me rude if I passed you without a word, my dear young lady. I was preoccupied with business matters.'

"I assured him that I was not offended. 'By the way,' said I, 'you seem to have quite a suite of spare rooms up there, and one of them has the shutters up.'

"He looked surprised and, as it seemed to me, a little startled at my remark.

"'Photography is one of my hobbies,' said he. 'I have made my dark room up there. But, dear me! what an observant young lady we have come upon. Who would have believed it? Who would have ever believed it?' He spoke in a jesting tone, but there was no jest in his eyes as he looked at me. I read suspicion there and annoyance, but no jest.

"Well, Mr. Holmes, from the moment that I understood that there was something about that suite of rooms which I was not to know, I was all on fire to go over them. It was not mere curiosity, though I have my share of that. It was more a feeling of duty, a feeling that some good might come from my penetrating to this place. They talk of woman's instinct; perhaps it was woman's instinct which gave me that feeling. At any rate, it was there, and I was keenly on the lookout for any chance to pass the forbidden door.

"It was only yesterday that the chance came. I may tell you that, besides Mr. Rucastle, both Toller and his wife find something to do in these deserted rooms, and I once saw him carrying a large black linen bag with him through the door. Recently he has been drinking hard, and yesterday evening he was very drunk; and when I came upstairs there was the key in the door. I have no doubt at all that he had left it there. Mr. and Mrs. Rucastle were both downstairs, and the child was with them, so that I had an admirable opportunity. I turned the key gently in the lock, opened the door, and slipped through.

"There was a little passage in front of me, unpapered and uncarpeted, which turned at a right angle at the farther end. Round this corner were three doors in a line, the first and third of which were open. They each led into an empty room, dusty and cheerless, with two windows in the one and one in the other, so thick with dirt that the evening light glimmered dimly through them. The centre door was closed, and across the outside of it had been fastened one of the broad bars of an iron bed, padlocked at one end to a ring in the wall, and fastened at the other with stout cord. The door itself was locked as well, and the key was not there. This barricaded door corresponded clearly with the shuttered window outside, and yet I could see by the glimmer from beneath it that the room was not in darkness. Evidently there was a skylight which let in light from above. As I stood in the passage gazing at the sinister door and wondering what secret it might veil, I suddenly heard the sound of steps within the room and saw a shadow pass backward and forward against the little slit of dim light which shone out from under the door. A mad, unreasoning terror rose up in me at the sight, Mr. Holmes. My overstrung nerves failed me suddenly, and I turned and ran, ran as though some dreadful hand were behind me clutching at the skirt of my dress. I rushed down the passage, through the door, and straight into the arms of Mr. Rucastle, who was waiting outside.

"'So,' said he, smiling, 'it was you, then. I thought that it must be when I saw the door open.'

"'Oh, I am so frightened!' I panted.

"'My dear young lady! my dear young lady!' you cannot think how caressing and soothing his manner was, 'and what has frightened you, my dear young lady?'

"But his voice was just a little too coaxing. He overdid it. I was keenly on my guard against him.

"'I was foolish enough to go into the empty wing,' I answered. 'But it is so lonely and eerie in this dim light that I was frightened and ran out again. Oh, it is so dreadfully still in there!'

"'Only that?' said he, looking at me keenly.

"'Why, what did you think?' I asked.

"'Why do you think that I lock this door?'

"'I am sure that I do not know.'

"'It is to keep people out who have no business there. Do you see?' He was still smiling in the most amiable manner.

"'I am sure if I had known'

"'Well, then, you know now. And if you ever put your foot over that threshold again', here in an instant the smile hardened into a grin of rage, and he glared down at me with the face of a demon 'I'll throw you to the mastiff.'

"I was so terrified that I do not know what I did. I suppose that I must have rushed past him into my room. I remember nothing until I found myself lying on my bed trembling all over. Then I thought of you, Mr. Holmes. I could not live there longer without some advice. I was frightened of the house, of the man of the woman, of the servants, even of the child. They were all horrible to me. If I could only bring you down all would be well. Of course I might have fled from the house, but my curiosity was almost as strong as my fears. My mind was soon made up. I would send you a wire. I put on my hat and cloak, went down to the office, which is about half a mile from the house, and then returned, feeling very much easier. A horrible doubt came into my mind as I approached the door lest the dog might be loose, but I remembered that Toller had drunk himself into a state of insensibility that evening, and I knew that he was the only one in the household who had any influence with the savage creature, or who would venture to set him free. I slipped in in safety and lay awake half the night in my joy at the thought of seeing you. I had no difficulty in getting leave to come into Winchester this morning, but I must be back before three o'clock, for Mr. and Mrs. Rucastle are going on a visit, and will be away all the evening, so that I must look after the child. Now I have told you all my adventures, Mr. Holmes, and I should be very glad if you could tell me what it all means, and, above all, what I should do."

Holmes and I had listened spellbound to this extraordinary story. My friend rose now and paced up and down the room, his hands in his pockets, and an expression of the most profound gravity upon his face.

"Is Toller still drunk?" he asked.

"Yes. I heard his wife tell Mrs. Rucastle that she could do nothing with him."

"That is well. And the Rucastles go out to-night?"

"Yes."

"Is there a cellar with a good strong lock?"

"Yes, the wine-cellar."

"You seem to me to have acted all through this matter like a very brave and sensible girl, Miss Hunter. Do you think that you could perform one more feat? I should not ask it of you if I did not think you a quite exceptional woman."

"I will try. What is it?"

"We shall be at the Copper Beeches by seven o'clock, my friend and I. The Rucastles will be gone by that time, and Toller will, we hope, be incapable. There only remains Mrs. Toller, who might give the alarm. If you could send her into the cellar on some errand, and then turn the key upon her, you would facilitate matters immensely."

"I will do it."

"Excellent! We shall then look thoroughly into the affair. Of course there is only one feasible explanation. You have been brought there to personate someone, and the real person is imprisoned in this chamber. That is obvious. As to who this prisoner is, I have no doubt that it is the daughter, Miss Alice Rucastle, if I remember right, who was said to have gone to America. You were chosen, doubtless, as resembling her in height, figure, and the color of your hair. Hers had been cut off, very possibly in some illness through which she has passed, and so, of course, yours had to be sacrificed also. By a curious chance you came upon her tresses. The man in the road was undoubtedly some friend of hers, possibly her fiancé, and no doubt, as you wore the girl's dress and were so like her, he was convinced from your laughter, whenever he saw you, and afterwards from your gesture, that Miss Rucastle was perfectly happy, and that she no longer desired his attentions. The dog is let loose at night to prevent him from endeavoring to communicate with her. So much is fairly clear. The most serious point in the case is the disposition of the child."

"What on earth has that to do with it?" I ejaculated.

"My dear Watson, you as a medical man are continually gaining light as to the tendencies of a child by the study of the parents. Don't you see that the converse is equally valid. I have frequently gained my first real insight into the character of parents by studying their children. This child's disposition is abnormally cruel, merely for cruelty's sake, and whether he derives this from his smiling father, as I should suspect, or from his mother, it bodes evil for the poor girl who is in their power."

"I am sure that you are right, Mr. Holmes," cried our client. "A thousand things come back to me which make me certain that you have hit it. Oh, let us lose not an instant in bringing help to this poor creature."

"We must be circumspect, for we are dealing with a very cunning man. We can do nothing until seven o'clock. At that hour we shall be with you, and it will not be long before we solve the mystery."

We were as good as our word, for it was just seven when we reached the Copper Beeches, having put up our trap at a wayside public-house. The group of trees, with their dark leaves shining like burnished metal in the light of the setting sun, were sufficient to mark the house even had Miss Hunter not been standing smiling on the door-step.

"Have you managed it?" asked Holmes.

A loud thudding noise came from somewhere downstairs. "That is Mrs. Toller in the cellar," said she. "Her husband lies snoring on the kitchen rug. Here are his keys, which are the duplicates of Mr. Rucastle's."

"You have done well indeed!" cried Holmes with enthusiasm. "Now lead the way, and we shall soon see the end of this black business."

We passed up the stair, unlocked the door, followed on down a passage, and found ourselves in front of the barricade which Miss Hunter had described. Holmes cut the cord and removed the transverse bar. Then he tried the various keys in the lock, but without success. No sound came from within, and at the silence Holmes's face clouded over.

"I trust that we are not too late," said he. "I think, Miss Hunter, that we had better go in without you. Now, Watson, put your shoulder to it, and we shall see whether we cannot make our way in."

It was an old rickety door and gave at once before our united strength. Together we rushed into the room. It was empty. There was no furniture save a little pallet bed, a small table, and a basketful of linen. The skylight above was open, and the prisoner gone.

"There has been some villainy here," said Holmes; "this beauty has guessed Miss Hunter's intentions and has carried his victim off."

"But how?"

"Through the skylight. We shall soon see how he managed it." He swung himself up onto the roof. "Ah, yes," he cried, "here's the end of a long light ladder against the eaves. That is how he did it."

"But it is impossible," said Miss Hunter; "the ladder was not there when the Rucastles went away."

"He has come back and done it. I tell you that he is a clever and dangerous man. I should not be very much surprised if this were he whose step I hear now upon the stair. I think, Watson, that it would be as well for you to have your pistol ready."

The words were hardly out of his mouth before a man appeared at the door of the room, a very fat and burly man, with a heavy stick in his hand. Miss Hunter screamed and shrunk against the wall at the sight of him, but Sherlock Holmes sprang forward and confronted him.

"You villain!" said he, "where's your daughter?"

The fat man cast his eyes round, and then up at the open skylight.

"It is for me to ask you that," he shrieked, "you thieves! Spies and thieves! I have caught you, have I? You are in my power. I'll serve you!" He turned and clattered down the stairs as hard as he could go.

"He's gone for the dog!" cried Miss Hunter.

"I have my revolver," said I.

"Better close the front door," cried Holmes, and we all rushed down the stairs together. We had hardly reached the hall when we heard the baying of a hound, and then a scream of agony, with a horrible worrying sound which it was dreadful to listen to. An elderly man with a red face and shaking limbs came staggering out at a side door.

"My God!" he cried. "Someone has loosed the dog. It's not been fed for two days. Quick, quick, or it'll be too late!"

Holmes and I rushed out and round the angle of the house, with Toller hurrying behind us. There was the huge famished brute, its black muzzle buried in Rucastle's throat, while he writhed and screamed upon the ground. Running up, I blew its brains out, and it fell over with its keen white teeth still meeting in the great creases of his neck. With much labour we separated them and carried him, living but horribly mangled, into the house. We laid him upon the drawing-room sofa, and having dispatched the sobered Toller to bear the news to his wife, I did what I could to relieve his pain. We were all assembled round him when the door opened, and a tall, gaunt woman entered the room.

"Mrs. Toller!" cried Miss Hunter.

"Yes, miss. Mr. Rucastle let me out when he came back before he went up to you. Ah, miss, it is a pity you didn't let me know what you were planning, for I would have told you that your pains were wasted."

"Ha!" said Holmes, looking keenly at her. "It is clear that Mrs. Toller knows more about this matter than anyone else."

"Yes, sir, I do, and I am ready enough to tell what I know."

"Then, pray, sit down, and let us hear it for there are several points on which I must confess that I am still in the dark."

"I will soon make it clear to you," said she; "and I'd have done so before now if I could ha' got out from the cellar. If there's police-court business over this, you'll remember that I was the one that stood your friend, and that I was Miss Alice's friend too.

"She was never happy at home, Miss Alice wasn't, from the time that her father married again. She was slighted like and had no say in anything, but it never really became bad for her until after she met Mr. Fowler at a friend's house. As well as I could learn, Miss Alice had rights of her own by will, but she was so quiet and patient, she was, that she never said a word about them but just left everything in Mr. Rucastle's hands. He knew he was safe with her; but when there was a chance of a husband coming forward, who would ask for all that the law would give him, then her father thought it time to put a stop on it. He wanted her to sign a paper, so that whether she married or not, he could use her money. When she wouldn't do it, he kept on worrying her until she got brain-fever, and for six weeks was at death's door. Then she got better at last, all worn to a shadow, and with her beautiful hair cut off; but that didn't make no change in her young man, and he stuck to her as true as man could be."

"Ah," said Holmes, "I think that what you have been good enough to tell us makes the matter fairly clear, and that I can deduce all that remains. Mr. Rucastle then, I presume, took to this system of imprisonment?"

"Yes, sir."

"And brought Miss Hunter down from London in order to get rid of the disagreeable persistence of Mr. Fowler."

"That was it, sir."

"But Mr. Fowler being a persevering man, as a good seaman should be, blockaded the house, and having met you succeeded by certain arguments, metallic or otherwise, in convincing you that your interests were the same as his."

"Mr. Fowler was a very kind-spoken, free-handed gentleman," said Mrs. Toller serenely.

"And in this way he managed that your good man should have no want of drink, and that a ladder should be ready at the moment when your master had gone out."

"You have it, sir, just as it happened."

"I am sure we owe you an apology, Mrs. Toller," said Holmes, "for you have certainly cleared up everything which puzzled us. And here comes the country surgeon and Mrs. Rucastle, so I think. Watson, that we had best escort Miss Hunter back to Winchester, as it seems to me that our locus standi now is rather a questionable one."

And thus was solved the mystery of the sinister house with the copper beeches in front of the door. Mr. Rucastle survived, but was always a broken man, kept alive solely through the care of his devoted wife. They still live with their old servants, who probably know so much of Rucastle's past life that he finds it difficult to part from them. Mr. Fowler and Miss Rucastle were married, by special license, in Southampton the day after their flight, and he is now the holder of a government appointment in the island of Mauritius. As to Miss Violet Hunter, my friend Holmes, rather to my disappointment, manifested no further interest in her when once she had ceased to be the centre of one of his problems, and she is now the head of a private school at Walsall, where I believe that she has met with considerable success.

The Black Doctor by Arthur Conan Doyle

Bishop's Crossing is a small village lying ten miles in a south-westerly direction from Liverpool. Here in the early seventies there settled a doctor named Aloysius Lana. Nothing was known locally either of his antecedents or of the reasons which had prompted him to come to this Lancashire hamlet. Two facts only were certain about him; the one that he had gained his medical qualification with some distinction at Glasgow; the other that he came undoubtedly of a tropical race, and was so dark that he might almost have had a strain of the Indian in his composition. His predominant features were, however, European, and he possessed a stately courtesy and carriage which suggested a Spanish extraction. A swarthy skin, raven-black hair, and dark, sparkling eyes under a pair of heavily-tufted brows made a strange contrast to the flaxen or chestnut rustics of England, and the newcomer was soon known as "The Black Doctor of Bishop's Crossing." At first it was a term of ridicule and reproach; as the years went on it became a title of honour which was familiar to the whole countryside, and extended far beyond the narrow confines of the village.

For the newcomer proved himself to be a capable surgeon and an accomplished physician. The practice of that district had been in the hands of Edward Rowe, the son of Sir William Rowe, the Liverpool consultant, but he had not inherited the talents of his father, and Dr. Lana, with his advantages of presence and of manner, soon beat him out of the field. Dr. Lana's social success was as rapid as his professional. A remarkable surgical cure in the case of the Hon. James

Lowry, the second son of Lord Belton, was the means of introducing him to county society, where he became a favourite through the charm of his conversation and the elegance of his manners. An absence of antecedents and of relatives is sometimes an aid rather than an impediment to social advancement, and the distinguished individuality of the handsome doctor was its own recommendation.

His patients had one fault - and one fault only - to find with him. He appeared to be a confirmed bachelor. This was the more remarkable since the house which he occupied was a large one, and it was known that his success in practice had enabled him to save considerable sums. At first the local matchmakers were continually coupling his name with one or other of the eligible ladies, but as years passed and Dr. Lana remained unmarried, it came to be generally understood that for some reason he must remain a bachelor. Some even went so far as to assert that he was already married, and that it was in order to escape the consequence of an early misalliance that he had buried himself at Bishop's Crossing. And, then, just as the matchmakers had finally given him up in despair, his engagement was suddenly announced to Miss Frances Morton, of Leigh Hall.

Miss Morton was a young lady who was well known upon the country-side, her father, James Haldane Morton, having been the Squire of Bishop's Crossing. Both her parents were, however, dead, and she lived with her only brother, Arthur Morton, who had inherited the family estate. In person Miss Morton was tall and stately, and she was famous for her quick, impetuous nature and for her strength of character. She met Dr. Lana at a garden-party, and a friendship, which quickly ripened into love, sprang up between them. Nothing could exceed their devotion to each other. There was some discrepancy in age, he being thirty-seven, and she twenty-four; but, save in that one respect, there was no possible objection to be found with the match. The engagement was in February, and it was arranged that the marriage should take place in August.

Upon the 3rd of June Dr. Lana received a letter from abroad. In a small village the postmaster is also in a position to be the gossip-master, and Mr. Bankley, of Bishop's Crossing, had many of the secrets of his neighbours in his possession. Of this particular letter he remarked only that it was in a curious envelope, that it was in a man's handwriting, that the postscript was Buenos Ayres, and the stamp of the Argentine Republic. It was the first letter which he had ever known Dr. Lana to have from abroad and this was the reason why his attention was particularly called to it before he handed it to the local postman. It was delivered by the evening delivery of that date.

Next morning - that is, upon the 4th of June - Dr. Lana called upon Miss Morton, and a long interview followed, from which he was observed to return in a state of great agitation. Miss Morton remained in her room all that day, and her maid found her several times in tears. In the course of a week it was an open secret to the whole village that the engagement was at an end, that Dr. Lana had behaved shamefully to the young lady, and that Arthur Morton, her brother, was talking of horse-whipping him. In what particular respect the doctor had behaved badly was unknown - some surmised one thing and some another; but it was observed, and taken as the obvious sign of a guilty conscience, that he would go for miles round rather than pass the windows of Leigh Hall, and that he gave up attending morning service upon Sundays where he might have met the young lady. There was an advertisement also in the Lancet as to the sale of a practice which mentioned no names, but which was thought by some to refer to Bishop's Crossing, and to mean that Dr. Lana was thinking of abandoning the scene of his success. Such was the position of affairs when, upon the evening of Monday, June 21st, there came a fresh development which changed what had been a mere village scandal into a tragedy which arrested the attention of the whole nation. Some detail is necessary to cause the facts of that evening to present their full significance.

The sole occupants of the doctor's house were his housekeeper, an elderly and most respectable woman, named Martha Woods, and a young servant - Mary Pilling. The coachman and the surgery-boy slept out. It was the custom of the doctor to sit at night in his study, which was next the surgery in the wing of the house which was farthest from the servants' quarters. This side of the house had a door of its own for the convenience of patients, so that it was possible for the doctor to admit and receive a visitor there without the knowledge of anyone. As a matter of fact, when patients came late it was quite usual for him to let them in and out by the surgery entrance, for the maid and the housekeeper were in the habit of retiring early.

On this particular night Martha Woods went into the doctor's study at half-past nine, and found him writing at his desk. She bade him good night, sent the maid to bed, and then occupied herself until a quarter to eleven in household matters. It was striking eleven upon the hall clock when she went to her own room. She had been there about a quarter of an hour or twenty minutes when she heard a cry or call, which appeared to come from within the house. She waited some time, but it was not repeated. Much alarmed, for the sound was loud and urgent, she put on a dressing-gown, and ran at the top of her speed to the doctor's study.

"Who's there?" cried a voice, as she tapped at the door.

"I am here, sir - Mrs. Woods."

"I beg that you will leave me in peace. Go back to your room this instant!" cried the voice, which was, to the best of her belief, that of her master. The tone was so harsh and so unlike her master's usual manner, that she was surprised and hurt.

"I thought I heard you calling, sir," she explained, but no answer was given to her. Mrs. Woods looked at the clock as she returned to her room, and it was then half-past eleven.

At some period between eleven and twelve (she could not be positive as to the exact hour) a patient called upon the doctor and was unable to get any reply from him. This late visitor was Mrs. Madding, the wife of the village grocer, who was dangerously ill of typhoid fever. Dr. Lana had asked her to look in the last thing and let him know how her husband was progressing. She observed that the light was burning in the study, but having knocked several times at the surgery door without response, she concluded that the doctor had been called out, and so returned home.

There is a short, winding drive with a lamp at the end of it leading down from the house to the road. As Mrs. Madding emerged from the gate a man was coming along the footpath. Thinking that it might be Dr. Lana returning from some professional visit, she waited for him, and was surprised to see that it was Mr. Arthur Morton, the young squire. In the light of the lamp she observed that his manner was excited, and that he carried in his hand a heavy hunting-crop. He was turning in at the gate when she addressed him.

"The doctor is not in, sir," said she.

"How do you know that?" he asked harshly.

"I have been to the surgery door, sir."

"I see a light," said the young squire, looking up the drive. "That is in his study, is it not?"

"Yes, sir; but I am sure that he is out."

"Well, he must come in again," said young Morton, and passed through the gate while Mrs. Madding went upon her homeward way.

At three o'clock that morning her husband suffered a sharp relapse, and she was so alarmed by his symptoms that she determined to call the doctor without delay. As she passed through the gate she was surprised to see someone lurking among the laurel bushes. It was certainly a man, and to the best of her belief Mr. Arthur Morton. Preoccupied with her own troubles, she gave no particular attention to the incident, but hurried on upon her errand.

When she reached the house she perceived to her surprise that the light was still burning in the study. She therefore tapped at the surgery door. There was no answer. She repeated the knocking several times without effect. It appeared to her to be unlikely that the doctor would either go to bed or go out leaving so brilliant a light behind him, and it struck Mrs. Madding that it was possible that he might have dropped asleep in his chair. She tapped at the study window, therefore, but without result. Then, finding that there was an opening between the curtain and the woodwork, she looked through.

The small room was brilliantly lighted from a large lamp on the central table, which was littered with the doctor's books and instruments. No one was visible, nor did she see anything unusual, except that in the farther shadow thrown by the table a dingy white glove was lying upon the carpet. And then suddenly, as her eyes became more accustomed to the light, a boot emerged from the other end of the shadow, and she realized, with a thrill of horror, that what she had taken to be a glove was the hand of a man, who was prostrate upon the floor. Understanding that something terrible had occurred, she rang at the front door, roused Mrs. Woods, the housekeeper, and the two women made their way into the study, having first dispatched the maidservant to the police-station.

At the side of the table, away from the window, Dr. Lana was discovered stretched upon his back and quite dead. It was evident that he had been subjected to violence, for one of his eyes was blackened and there were marks of bruises about his face and neck. A slight thickening and swelling of his features appeared to suggest that the cause of his death had been strangulation. He was dressed in his usual professional clothes, but wore cloth slippers, the soles of which were perfectly clean. The carpet was marked all over, especially on the side of the door, with traces of dirty boots, which were presumably left by the murderer. It was evident that someone had entered by the surgery door, had killed the doctor, and had then made his escape unseen. That the assailant was a man was certain, from the size of the footprints and from the nature of the injuries. But beyond that point the police found it very difficult to go.

There were no signs of robbery, and the doctor's gold watch was safe in his pocket. He kept a heavy cash-box in the room, and this was discovered to be locked but empty. Mrs. Woods had an impression that a large sum was usually kept there, but the doctor had paid a heavy corn bill in cash only that very day, and it was conjectured that it was to this and not to a robber that the emptiness of the box was due. One thing in the room was missing - but that one thing was suggestive. The portrait of Miss Morton, which had always stood upon the side-table, had been taken from its frame, and carried off. Mrs. Woods had observed it there when she waited upon her employer that evening, and now it was gone. On the other hand, there was picked up from the floor a green eye-patch, which the housekeeper could not remember to have seen before. Such a patch might, however, be in the possession of a doctor, and there was nothing to indicate that it was in any way connected with the crime.

Suspicion could only turn in one direction, and Arthur Morton, the young squire, was immediately arrested. The evidence against him was circumstantial, but damning. He was devoted to his sister, and it was shown that since the rupture between her and Dr. Lana he had been heard again and again to express himself in the most vindictive terms towards her former lover. He had, as stated, been seen somewhere about eleven o'clock entering the doctor's drive with a hunting-crop in his hand. He had then, according to the theory of the police, broken in upon the doctor, whose exclamation of fear or of anger had been loud enough to attract the attention of Mrs. Woods. When Mrs. Woods descended, Dr. Lana had made up his mind to talk it over with his visitor, and had, therefore, sent his housekeeper back to her room. This conversation had lasted a long time, had become more and more fiery, and had ended by a personal struggle, in which the doctor lost his life. The fact, revealed by a post-mortem, that his heart was much diseased - an ailment quite unsuspected during his life - would make it possible that death might in his case ensue from injuries which would not be fatal to a healthy man. Arthur Morton had then removed his sister's photograph, and had made his way homeward, stepping aside into the laurel bushes to avoid Mrs. Madding at the gate. This was the theory of the prosecution, and the case which they presented was a formidable one.

On the other hand, there were some strong points for the defence. Morton was high-spirited and impetuous, like his sister, but he was respected and liked by everyone, and his frank and honest nature seemed to be incapable of such a crime. His own explanation was that he was anxious to have a conversation with Dr. Lana about some urgent family matters (from first to last he refused even to mention the name of his sister). He did not attempt to deny that this conversation would probably have been of an unpleasant nature. He had heard from a patient that the doctor was out, and he therefore waited until about three in the morning for his return, but as he had seen nothing of him up to that hour, he had given it up and had returned home. As to his death, he knew no more about it than the constable who arrested him. He had formerly been an intimate friend of the deceased man; but circumstances, which he would prefer not to mention, had brought about a change in his sentiments.

There were several facts which supported his innocence. It was certain that Dr. Lana was alive and in his study at half-past eleven o'clock. Mrs. Woods was prepared to swear that it was at that hour that she had heard his voice. The friends of the prisoner contended that it was probable that at that time Dr. Lana was not alone. The sound which had originally attracted the attention of the housekeeper, and her master's unusual impatience that she should leave him in peace, seemed to point to that. If this were so then it appeared to be probable that he had met his end between the moment when the housekeeper heard his voice and the time when Mrs. Madding made her first call and found it impossible to attract his attention. But if this were the time of his death, then it was certain that Mr. Arthur Morton could not be guilty, as it was after this that she had met the young squire at the gate.

If this hypothesis were correct, and someone was with Dr. Lana before Mrs. Madding met Mr. Arthur Morton, then who was this someone, and what motives had he for wishing evil to the doctor? It was universally admitted that if the friends of the accused could throw light upon this, they would have gone a long way towards establishing his innocence. But in the meanwhile it was open to the public to say - as they did say - that there was no proof that anyone had been there at all except the young squire; while, on the other hand, there was ample proof that his motives in going were of a sinister kind. When Mrs. Madding called, the doctor might have retired to his room, or he might, as she thought at the time, have gone out and returned afterwards to find Mr. Arthur Morton waiting for him. Some of the supporters of the accused laid stress upon the fact that the photograph of his sister Frances, which had been removed from the doctor's room, had not been found in her brother's possession. This argument, however, did not count for much, as he had ample time before his arrest to burn it or to destroy it. As to the only positive evidence in the case - the muddy footmarks upon the floor - they were so blurred by the softness of the carpet that it was impossible to make any trustworthy deduction from them. The most that could be said was that their appearance was not inconsistent with the theory that they were made by the accused, and it was further shown that his boots were very muddy upon that night. There had been a heavy shower in the afternoon, and all boots were probably in the same condition.

Such is a bald statement of the singular and romantic series of events which centred public attention upon this Lancashire tragedy. The unknown origin of the doctor, his curious and distinguished personality, the position of the man who was accused of the murder, and the love affair which had preceded the crimes all combined to make the affair one of those dramas which absorb the whole interest of a nation. Throughout the three kingdoms men discussed the case of the Black Doctor of Bishop's Crossing, and many were the theories put forward to explain the facts; but it may safely be said that among them all there was not one which prepared the minds of the public for the extraordinary sequel, which caused so much excitement upon the first day of the trial, and came to a climax upon the second. The long files of the Lancaster Weekly with their report of the case lie before me as I write, but I must content myself with a synopsis of the case up to the point when, upon the evening of the first day, the evidence of Miss Frances Morton threw a singular light upon the case.

Mr. Porlock Carr, the counsel for the prosecution, had marshalled his facts with his usual skill, and as the day wore on, it became more and more evident how difficult was the task which Mr. Humphrey, who had been retained for the defence, had before him. Several witnesses were put up to swear to the intemperate expressions which the young squire had been heard to utter about the doctor, and the fiery manner in which he resented the alleged ill-treatment of his sister. Mrs. Madding repeated her evidence as to the visit which had been paid late at night by the prisoner to the deceased, and it was shown by another witness that the prisoner was aware that the doctor was in the habit of sitting up alone in this isolated wing of the house, and that he had chosen this very late hour to call because he knew that his victim would then be at his mercy. A servant at the squire's house was compelled to admit that he had heard his master return about three that morning, which corroborated Mrs. Madding's statement that she had seen him among the laurel bushes near the gate upon the occasion of her second visit. The muddy boots and an alleged similarity in the footprints were duly dwelt upon, and it was felt when the case for the prosecution had been presented that, however circumstantial it might be, it was none the less so complete and so convincing, that the fate of the prisoner was sealed, unless something quite unexpected should be disclosed by the defence. It was three o'clock when the prosecution closed. At half-past four, when the court rose, a new and unlooked-for development had occurred. I extract the incident, or part of it, from the journal which I have already mentioned, omitting the preliminary observations of the counsel.

Considerable sensation was caused in the crowded court when the first witness called for the defence proved to be Miss Frances Morton, the sister of the prisoner. Our readers will remember that the young lady had been engaged to Dr. Lana, and that it was his anger over the sudden termination of this engagement which was thought to have driven her brother to the perpetration of this crime. Miss Morton had not, however, been directly implicated in the case in any way, either at the inquest or at the police-court proceedings, and her appearance as the leading witness for the defence came as a surprise upon the public.

Miss Frances Morton, who was a tall and handsome brunette, gave her evidence in a low but clear voice, though it was evident throughout that she was suffering from extreme emotion. She alluded to her engagement to the doctor, touched briefly upon its termination, which was due, she said, to personal matters connected with his family, and surprised the court by asserting that she had always considered her brother's resentment to be unreasonable and intemperate. In answer to a direct question from her counsel, she replied that she did not feel that she had any grievance whatever against Dr. Lana, and that in her opinion he had acted in a perfectly honourable manner. Her brother, on an insufficient knowledge of the facts, had taken another view, and she was compelled to acknowledge that, in spite of her entreaties, he had uttered threats of personal violence against the doctor, and had, upon the evening of the tragedy, announced his intention of "having it out with him." She had done her best to bring him to a more reasonable frame of mind, but he was very headstrong where his emotions or prejudices were concerned.

Up to this point the young lady's evidence had appeared to make against the prisoner rather than in his favour. The questions of her counsel, however, soon put a very different light upon the matter, and disclosed an unexpected line of defence.

Mr. Humphrey: Do you believe your brother to be guilty of this crime?

The Judge: I cannot permit that question, Mr. Humphrey. We are here to decide upon questions of fact - not of belief.

Mr. Humphrey: Do you know that your brother is not guilty of the death of Doctor Lana?

Miss Morton: Yes.

Mr. Humphrey: How do you know it?

Miss Morton: Because Dr. Lana is not dead.

There followed a prolonged sensation in court, which interrupted the examination of the witness.

Mr. Humphrey: And how do you know, Miss Morton, that Dr. Lana is not dead?

Miss Morton: Because I have received a letter from him since the date of his supposed death.

Mr. Humphrey: Have you this letter?

Miss Morton: Yes, but I should prefer not to show it.

Mr. Humphrey: Have you the envelope?

Miss Morton: Yes, it is here.

Mr. Humphrey: What is the post-mark?

Miss Morton: Liverpool.

Mr. Humphrey: And the date?

Miss Morton: June the 22nd.

Mr. Humphrey: That being the day after his alleged death. Are you prepared to swear to this handwriting, Miss Morton?

Miss Morton: Certainly.

Mr. Humphrey: I am prepared to call six other witnesses, my lord, to testify that this letter is in the writing of Doctor Lana.

The Judge: Then you must call them tomorrow.

Mr. Porlock Carr (counsel for the prosecution): In the meantime, my lord, we claim possession of this document, so that we may obtain expert evidence as to how far it is an imitation of the handwriting of the gentleman whom we still confidently assert to be deceased. I need not point out that the theory so unexpectedly sprung upon us may prove to be a very obvious device adopted by the friends of the prisoner in order to divert this inquiry. I would draw attention to the fact that the young lady must, according to her own account, have possessed this letter during the proceedings at the inquest and at the police-court. She desires us to believe that she permitted these to proceed, although she held in her pocket evidence which would at any moment have brought them to an end.

Mr. Humphrey. Can you explain this, Miss Morton?

Miss Morton: Dr. Lana desired his secret to be preserved.

Mr. Porlock Carr: Then why have you made this public?

Miss Morton: To save my brother.

A murmur of sympathy broke out in court, which was instantly suppressed by the Judge.

The Judge: Admitting this line of defence, it lies with you, Mr. Humphrey, to throw a light upon who this man is whose body has been recognized by so many friends and patients of Dr. Lana as being that of the doctor himself.

A Juryman: Has anyone up to now expressed any doubt about the matter?

Mr. Porlock Carr: Not to my knowledge.

Mr. Humphrey: We hope to make the matter clear.

The Judge: Then the court adjourns until tomorrow.

This new development of the case excited the utmost interest among the general public. Press comment was prevented by the fact that the trial was still undecided, but the question was everywhere argued as to how far there could be truth in Miss Morton's declaration, and how far it might be a daring ruse for the purpose of saving her brother. The obvious dilemma in which the missing doctor stood was that if by any extraordinary chance he was not dead, then he must be held responsible for the death of this unknown man, who resembled him so exactly, and who was found in his study. This letter which Miss Morton refused to produce was possibly a confession of guilt, and she might find herself in the terrible position of only being able to save her brother from the gallows by the sacrifice of her former lover. The court next morning was crammed to overflowing, and a murmur of excitement passed over it when Mr. Humphrey was observed to enter in a state of emotion, which even his trained nerves could not conceal, and to confer with the opposing counsel. A few hurried words - words which left a look of amazement upon Mr. Porlock Carr's face - passed between them, and then the counsel for the defence, addressing the Judge, announced that, with the consent of the prosecution, the young lady who had given evidence upon the sitting before would not be recalled.

The Judge: But you appear, Mr. Humphrey, to have left matters in a very unsatisfactory state.

Mr. Humphrey: Perhaps, my lord, my next witness may help to clear them up.

The Judge: Then call your next witness.

Mr. Humphrey: I call Dr. Aloysius Lana.

The learned counsel has made many telling remarks in his day, but he has certainly never produced such a sensation with so short a sentence. The court was simply stunned with amazement as the very man whose fate had been the subject of so much contention appeared bodily before them in the witness-box. Those among the spectators who had known him at Bishop's Crossing saw him now, gaunt and thin, with deep lines of care upon his face. But in spite of his melancholy bearing and despondent expression, there were few who could say that they had ever seen a man of more distinguished presence. Bowing to the judge, he asked if he might be allowed to make a statement, and having been duly informed that whatever he said might be used against him, he bowed once more, and proceeded:

"My wish," said he, "is to hold nothing back, but to tell with perfect frankness all that occurred upon the night of the 21st of June. Had I known that the innocent had suffered, and that so much trouble had been brought upon those whom I love best in the world, I should have come forward long ago; but there were reasons which prevented these things from coming to my ears. It was my desire that an unhappy man should vanish from the world which had known him, but I had not foreseen that others would be affected by my actions. Let me to the best of my ability repair the evil which I have done.

"To anyone who is acquainted with the history of the Argentine Republic the name of Lana is well known. My father, who came of the best blood of old Spain, filled all the highest offices of the State, and would have been President but for his death in the riots of San Juan. A brilliant career might have been open to my twin brother Ernest and myself had it not been for financial losses which made it necessary that we should earn our own living. I apologize, sir, if these details appear to be irrelevant, but they are a necessary introduction to that which is to follow.

"I had, as I have said, a twin brother named Ernest, whose resemblance to me was so great that even when we were together people could see no difference between us. Down to the smallest detail we were exactly the same. As we grew older this likeness became less marked because our expression was not the same, but with our features in repose the points of difference were very slight.

"It does not become me to say too much of one who is dead, the more so as he is my only brother, but I leave his character to those who knew him best. I will only say - for I haveto say it - that in my early manhood I conceived a horror of him, and that I had good reason for the aversion which filled me. My own reputation suffered from his actions, for our close resemblance caused me to be credited with many of them. Eventually, in a peculiarly disgraceful business, he contrived to throw the whole odium upon me in such a way that I was forced to leave the Argentine for ever, and to seek a career in Europe. The freedom from his hated presence more than compensated me for the loss of my native land. I had enough money to defray my medical studies at Glasgow, and I finally settled in practice at Bishop's Crossing, in the firm conviction that in that remote Lancashire hamlet I should never hear of him again.

"For years my hopes were fulfilled, and then at last he discovered me. Some Liverpool man who visited Buenos Ayres put him upon my track. He had lost all his money, and he thought that he would come over and share mine. Knowing my horror of him, he rightly thought that I would be willing to buy him off. I received a letter from him saying that he was coming. It was at a crisis in my own affairs, and his arrival might conceivably bring trouble, and even disgrace, upon some whom I was especially bound to shield from anything of the kind. I took steps to insure that any evil which might come should fall on me only, and that" - here he turned and looked at the prisoner - "was the cause of conduct upon my part which has been too harshly judged. My only motive was to screen those who were dear to me from any possible connection with scandal or disgrace. That scandal and disgrace would come with my brother was only to say that what had been would be again.

"My brother arrived himself one night not very long after my receipt of the letter. I was sitting in my study after the servants had gone to bed, when I heard a footstep upon the gravel outside, and an instant later I saw his face looking in at me through the window. He was a clean-shaven man like myself, and the resemblance between us was still so great that, for an instant, I thought it was my own reflection in the glass. He had a dark patch over his eye, but our features were absolutely the same. Then he smiled in a sardonic way which had been a trick of his from his boyhood, and I knew that he was the same brother who had driven me from my native land, and brought disgrace upon what had been an honourable name. I went to the door and I admitted him. That would be about ten o'clock that night.

"When he came into the glare of the lamp, I saw at once that he had fallen upon very evil days. He had walked from Liverpool, and he was tired and ill. I was quite shocked by the expression upon his face. My medical knowledge told me that there was some serious internal malady. He had been drinking also, and his face was bruised as the result of a scuffle which he had had with some sailors. It was to cover his injured eye that he wore this patch, which he removed when he entered the room. He was himself dressed in a pea-jacket and flannel shirt, and his feet were bursting through his boots. But his poverty had only made him more savagely vindictive towards me. His hatred rose to the height of a mania. I had been rolling in money in England, according to his account, while he had been starving in South America. I cannot describe to you the threats which he uttered or the insults which he poured upon me. My impression is, that hardships and debauchery had unhinged his reason. He paced about the room like a wild beast, demanding drink, demanding money, and all in the foulest language. I am a hot-tempered man, but I thank God that I am able to say that I remained master of myself, and that I never raised a hand against him. My coolness only irritated him the more. He raved, he cursed, he shook his fists in my face, and then suddenly a horrible spasm passed over his features, he clapped his hand to his side, and with a loud cry he fell in a heap at my feet. I raised him up and stretched him upon the sofa, but no answer came to my exclamations, and the hand which I held in mine was cold and clammy. His diseased heart had broken down. His own violence had killed him.

"For a long time I sat as if I were in some dreadful dream, staring at the body of my brother. I was aroused by the knocking of Mrs. Woods, who had been disturbed by that dying cry. I sent her away to bed. Shortly afterwards a patient tapped at the surgery door, but as I took no notice, he or she went off again. Slowly and gradually as I sat there a plan was forming itself in my head in the curious automatic way in which plans do form. When I rose from my chair my future movements were finally decided upon without my having been conscious of any process of thought. It was an instinct which irresistibly inclined me towards one course.

"Ever since that change in my affairs to which I have alluded, Bishop's Crossing had become hateful to me. My plans of life had been ruined, and I had met with hasty judgments and unkind treatment where I had expected sympathy. It is true that any danger of scandal from my brother had passed away with his life; but still, I was sore about the past, and felt that things could never be as they had been. It may be that I was unduly sensitive, and that I had not made sufficient allowance for others, but my feelings were as I describe. Any chance of getting away from Bishop's Crossing and of everyone in it would be most welcome to me. And here was such a chance as I could never have dared to hope for, a chance which would enable me to make a clean break with the past.

"There was this dead man lying upon the sofa, so like me that save for some little thickness and coarseness of the features there was no difference at all. No one had seen him come and no one would miss him. We were both clean-shaven, and his hair was about the same length as my own. If I changed clothes with him, then Dr. Aloysius Lana would be found lying dead in his study, and there would be an end of an unfortunate fellow, and of a blighted career. There was plenty of ready money in the room, and this I could carry away with me to help me to start once more in some other land. In my brother's clothes I could walk by night unobserved as far as Liverpool, and in that great seaport I would soon find some means of leaving the country. After my lost hopes, the humblest existence where I was unknown was far preferable, in my estimation, to a practice, however successful, in Bishop's Crossing, where at any moment I might come face to face with those whom I should wish, if it were possible, to forget. I determined to effect the change.

"And I did so. I will not go into particulars, for the recollection is as painful as the experience; but in an hour my brother lay, dressed down to the smallest detail in my clothes, while I slunk out by the surgery door, and taking the back path which led across some fields, I started off to make the best of my way to Liverpool, where I arrived the same night. My bag of money and a certain portrait were all I carried out of the house, and I left behind me in my hurry the shade which my brother had been wearing over his eye. Everything else of his I took with me.

"I give you my word, sir, that never for one instant did the idea occur to me that people might think that I had been murdered, nor did I imagine that anyone might be caused serious danger through this stratagem by which I endeavoured to gain a fresh start in the world. On the contrary, it was the thought of relieving others from the burden of my presence which was always uppermost in my mind. A sailing vessel was leaving Liverpool that very day for Corunna, and in this I took my passage, thinking that the voyage would give me time to recover my balance, and to consider the future. But before I left my resolution softened. I bethought me that there was one person in the world to whom I would not cause an hour of sadness. She would mourn me in her heart, however harsh and unsympathetic her relatives might be. She understood and appreciated the motives upon which I had acted, and if the rest of her family condemned me, she, at least, would not forget. And so I sent her a note under the seal of secrecy to save her from a baseless grief. If under the pressure of events she broke that seal, she has my entire sympathy and forgiveness.

"It was only last night that I returned to England, and during all this time I have heard nothing of the sensation which my supposed death had caused, nor of the accusation that Mr. Arthur Morton had been concerned in it. It was in a late evening paper that I read an account of the proceedings of yesterday, and I have come this morning as fast as an express train could bring me to testify to the truth."

Such was the remarkable statement of Dr. Aloysius Lana which brought the trial to a sudden termination. A subsequent investigation corroborated it to the extent of finding out the vessel in which his brother Ernest Lana had come over from South America. The ship's doctor was able to testify that he had complained of a weak heart during the voyage, and that his symptoms were consistent with such a death as was described.

As to Dr. Aloysius Lana, he returned to the village from which he had made so dramatic a disappearance, and a complete reconciliation was effected between him and the young squire, the latter having acknowledged that he had entirely misunderstood the other's motives in withdrawing from his engagement. That another reconciliation followed may be judged from a notice extracted from a prominent column in the Morning Post:

"A marriage was solemnized upon September 19th, by the Rev. Stephen Johnson, at the parish church of Bishop's Crossing, between Aloysius Xavier Lana, son of Don Alfredo Lana, formerly Foreign Minister of the Argentine Republic, and Frances Morton, only daughter of the late James Morton, J.P., of Leigh Hall, Bishop's Crossing, Lancashire."

The Bolted Door by Edith Wharton

I

Hubert Granice, pacing the length of his pleasant lamp-lit library, paused to compare his watch with the clock on the chimney-piece.

Three minutes to eight.

In exactly three minutes Mr. Peter Ascham, of the eminent legal firm of Ascham and Pettilow, would have his punctual hand on the door-bell of the flat. It was a comfort to reflect that Ascham was so punctual, the suspense was beginning to make his host nervous. And the sound of the door-bell would be the beginning of the end, after that there'd be no going back, by God, no going back!

Granice resumed his pacing. Each time he reached the end of the room opposite the door he caught his reflection in the Florentine mirror above the fine old walnut credence he had picked up at Dijon, saw himself spare, quick-moving, carefully brushed and dressed, but furrowed, gray about the temples, with a stoop which he corrected by a spasmodic straightening of the shoulders whenever a glass confronted him: a tired middle-aged man, baffled, beaten, worn out.

As he summed himself up thus for the third or fourth time the door opened and he turned with a thrill of relief to greet his guest. But it was only the man-servant who entered, advancing silently over the mossy surface of the old Turkey rug.

"Mr. Ascham telephones, sir, to say he's unexpectedly detained and can't be here till eight-thirty."

Granice made a curt gesture of annoyance. It was becoming harder and harder for him to control these reflexes. He turned on his heel, tossing to the servant over his shoulder: "Very good. Put off dinner."

Down his spine he felt the man's injured stare. Mr. Granice had always been so mild-spoken to his people, no doubt the odd change in his manner had already been noticed and discussed below stairs. And very likely they suspected the cause. He stood drumming on the writing-table till he heard the servant go out; then he threw himself into a chair, propping his elbows on the table and resting his chin on his locked hands.

Another half hour alone with it!

He wondered irritably what could have detained his guest. Some professional matter, no doubt the punctilious lawyer would have allowed nothing less to interfere with a dinner engagement, more especially since Granice, in his note, had said: "I shall want a little business chat afterward."

But what professional matter could have come up at that unprofessional hour? Perhaps some other soul in misery had called on the lawyer; and, after all, Granice's note had given no hint of his own need! No doubt Ascham thought he merely wanted to make another change in his will. Since he had come into his little property, ten years earlier, Granice had been perpetually tinkering with his will.

Suddenly another thought pulled him up, sending a flush to his sallow temples. He remembered a word he had tossed to the lawyer some six weeks earlier, at the Century Club. "Yes, my play's as good as taken. I shall be calling on you soon to go over the contract. Those theatrical chaps are so slippery, I won't trust anybody but you to tie the knot for me!" That, of course, was what Ascham would think he was wanted for. Granice, at the idea, broke into an audible laugh, a queer stage-laugh, like the cackle of a baffled villain in a melodrama. The absurdity, the unnaturalness of the sound abashed him, and he compressed his lips angrily. Would he take to soliloquy next?

He lowered his arms and pulled open the upper drawer of the writing-table. In the right-hand corner lay a thick manuscript, bound in paper folders, and tied with a string beneath which a letter had been slipped. Next to the manuscript was a small revolver. Granice stared a moment at these oddly associated objects; then he took the letter from under the string and slowly began to open it. He had known he should do so from the moment his hand touched the drawer. Whenever his eye fell on that letter some relentless force compelled him to re-read it.

It was dated about four weeks back, under the letter-head of "The Diversity Theatre."

"My Dear Mr. Granice:

"I have given the matter my best consideration for the last month, and it's no use the play won't do. I have talked it over with Miss Melrose and you know there isn't a gamer artist on our stage and I regret to tell you she feels just as I do about it. It isn't the poetry that scares her or me either. We both want to do all we can to help along the poetic drama, we believe the public's ready for it, and we're willing to take a big financial risk in order to be the first to give them what they want. But we don't believe they could be made to want this. The fact is, there isn't enough drama in your play to the allowance of poetry, the thing drags all through. You've got a big idea, but it's not out of swaddling clothes.

"If this was your first play I'd say: try again. But it has been just the same with all the others you've shown me. And you remember the result of 'The Lee Shore,' where you carried all the expenses of production yourself, and we couldn't fill the theatre for a week. Yet 'The Lee Shore' was a modern problem play, much easier to swing than blank verse. It isn't as if you hadn't tried all kinds"

Granice folded the letter and put it carefully back into the envelope. Why on earth was he re-reading it, when he knew every phrase in it by heart, when for a month past he had seen it, night after night, stand out in letters of flame against the darkness of his sleepless lids?

"It has been just the same with all the other you've shown me."

That was the way they dismissed ten years of passionate unremitting work!

"You remember the result of 'The Lee Shore'."

Good God, as if he were likely to forget it! He re-lived it all now in a drowning flash: the persistent rejection of the play, his sudden resolve to put it on at his own cost, to spend ten thousand dollars of his inheritance on testing his chance of success, the fever of preparation, the dry-mouthed agony of the "first night," the flat fall, the stupid press, his secret rush to Europe to escape the condolence of his friends!

"It isn't as if you hadn't tried all kinds."

No, he had tried all kinds: comedy, tragedy, prose and verse, the light curtain-raiser, the short sharp drama, the bourgeoisrealistic and the lyrical-romantic, finally deciding that he would no longer "prostitute his talent" to win popularity, but would impose on the public his own theory of art in the form of five acts of blank verse. Yes, he had offered them everything and always with the same result.

Ten years of it, ten years of dogged work and unrelieved failure. The ten years from forty to fifty, the best ten years of his life! And if one counted the years before, the silent years of dreams, assimilation, preparation, then call it half a man's life-time: half a man's life-time thrown away!

And what was he to do with the remaining half? Well, he had settled that, thank God! He turned and glanced anxiously at the clock. Ten minutes past eight, only ten minutes had been consumed in that stormy rush through his whole past! And he must wait another twenty minutes for Ascham. It was one of the worst symptoms of his case that, in proportion as he had grown to shrink from human company, he dreaded more and more to be alone. . . . But why the devil was he waiting for Ascham? Why didn't he cut the knot himself? Since he was so unutterably sick of the whole business, why did he have to call in an outsider to rid him of this nightmare of living?

He opened the drawer again and laid his hand on the revolver. It was a small slim ivory toy, just the instrument for a tired sufferer to give himself a "hypodermic" with. Granice raised it slowly in one hand, while with the other he felt under the thin hair at the back of his head, between the ear and the nape. He knew just where to place the muzzle: he had once got a young surgeon to show him. And as he found the spot, and lifted the revolver to it, the inevitable phenomenon occurred. The hand that held the weapon began to shake, the tremor communicated itself to his arm, his heart gave a wild leap which sent up a wave of deadly nausea to his throat, he smelt the powder, he sickened at the crash of the bullet through his skull, and a sweat of fear broke out over his forehead and ran down his quivering face. . .

He laid away the revolver with an oath and, pulling out a cologne-scented handkerchief, passed it tremulously over his brow and temples. It was no use, he knew he could never do it in that way. His attempts at self-destruction were as futile as his snatches at fame! He couldn't make himself a real life, and he couldn't get rid of the life he had. And that was why he had sent for Ascham to help him. . .

The lawyer, over the Camembert and Burgundy, began to excuse himself for his delay.

"I didn't like to say anything while your man was about but the fact is, I was sent for on a rather unusual matter"

"Oh, it's all right," said Granice cheerfully. He was beginning to feel the usual reaction that food and company produced. It was not any recovered pleasure in life that he felt, but only a deeper withdrawal into himself. It was easier to go on automatically with the social gestures than to uncover to any human eye the abyss within him.

"My dear fellow, it's sacrilege to keep a dinner waiting, especially the production of an artist like yours." Mr. Ascham sipped his Burgundy luxuriously. "But the fact is, Mrs. Ashgrove sent for me."

Granice raised his head with a quick movement of surprise. For a moment he was shaken out of his self-absorption.

"Mrs. Ashgrove?"

Ascham smiled. "I thought you'd be interested; I know your passion for causes celebres. And this promises to be one. Of course it's out of our line entirely, we never touch criminal cases. But she wanted to consult me as a friend. Ashgrove was a distant connection of my wife's. And, by Jove, it is a queer case!" The servant re-entered, and Ascham snapped his lips shut.

Would the gentlemen have their coffee in the dining-room?

"No, serve it in the library," said Granice, rising. He led the way back to the curtained confidential room. He was really curious to hear what Ascham had to tell him.

While the coffee and cigars were being served he fidgeted about the library, glancing at his letters, the usual meaningless notes and bills, and picking up the evening paper. As he unfolded it a headline caught his eye.

"ROSE MELROSE WANTS TO PLAY POETRY.

"THINKS SHE HAS FOUND HER POET."

He read on with a thumping heart, found the name of a young author he had barely heard of, saw the title of a play, a "poetic drama," dance before his eyes, and dropped the paper, sick, disgusted. It was true, then, she was "game" it was not the manner but the matter she mistrusted!

Granice turned to the servant, who seemed to be purposely lingering. "I shan't need you this evening, Flint. I'll lock up myself."

He fancied the man's acquiescence implied surprise. What was going on, Flint seemed to wonder, that Mr. Granice should want him out of the way? Probably he would find a pretext for coming back to see. Granice suddenly felt himself enveloped in a network of espionage.

As the door closed he threw himself into an armchair and leaned forward to take a light from Ascham's cigar.

"Tell me about Mrs. Ashgrove," he said, seeming to himself to speak stiffly, as if his lips were cracked.

"Mrs. Ashgrove? Well, there's not much to tell."

"And you couldn't if there were?" Granice smiled.

"Probably not. As a matter of fact, she wanted my advice about her choice of counsel. There was nothing especially confidential in our talk."

"And what's your impression, now you've seen her?"

"My impression is, very distinctly, that nothing will ever be known."

"Ah?" Granice murmured, puffing at his cigar.

"I'm more and more convinced that whoever poisoned Ashgrove knew his business, and will consequently never be found out. That's a capital cigar you've given me."

"You like it? I get them over from Cuba." Granice examined his own reflectively. "Then you believe in the theory that the clever criminals never are caught?"

"Of course I do. Look about you, look back for the last dozen years, none of the big murder problems are ever solved." The lawyer ruminated behind his blue cloud. "Why, take the instance in your own family: I'd forgotten I had an illustration at hand! Take old Joseph Lenman's murder, do you suppose that will ever be explained?"

As the words dropped from Ascham's lips his host looked slowly about the library, and every object in it stared back at him with a stale unescapable familiarity. How sick he was of looking at that room! It was as dull as the face of a wife one has wearied of. He cleared his throat slowly; then he turned his head to the lawyer and said: "I could explain the Lenman murder myself."

Ascham's eye kindled: he shared Granice's interest in criminal cases.

"By Jove! You've had a theory all this time? It's odd you never mentioned it. Go ahead and tell me. There are certain features in the Lenman case not unlike this Ashgrove affair, and your idea may be a help."

Granice paused and his eye reverted instinctively to the table drawer in which the revolver and the manuscript lay side by side. What if he were to try another appeal to Rose Melrose? Then he looked at the notes and bills on the table, and the horror of taking up again the lifeless routine of life, of performing the same automatic gestures another day, displaced his fleeting vision.

"I haven't a theory. I know who murdered Joseph Lenman."

Ascham settled himself comfortably in his chair, prepared for enjoyment.

"You know? Well, who did?" he laughed.

"I did," said Granice, rising.

He stood before Ascham, and the lawyer lay back staring up at him. Then he broke into another laugh.

"Why, this is glorious! You murdered him, did you? To inherit his money, I suppose? Better and better! Go on, my boy! Unbosom yourself! Tell me all about it! Confession is good for the soul."

Granice waited till the lawyer had shaken the last peal of laughter from his throat; then he repeated doggedly: "I murdered him."

The two men looked at each other for a long moment, and this time Ascham did not laugh.

"Granice!"

"I murdered him to get his money, as you say."

There was another pause, and Granice, with a vague underlying sense of amusement, saw his guest's look change from pleasantry to apprehension.

"What's the joke, my dear fellow? I fail to see."

"It's not a joke. It's the truth. I murdered him." He had spoken painfully at first, as if there were a knot in his throat; but each time he repeated the words he found they were easier to say.

Ascham laid down his extinct cigar.

"What's the matter? Aren't you well? What on earth are you driving at?"

"I'm perfectly well. But I murdered my cousin, Joseph Lenman, and I want it known that I murdered him."

"You want it known?"

"Yes. That's why I sent for you. I'm sick of living, and when I try to kill myself I funk it." He spoke quite naturally now, as if the knot in his throat had been untied.

"Good Lord, good Lord," the lawyer gasped.

"But I suppose," Granice continued, "there's no doubt this would be murder in the first degree? I'm sure of the chair if I own up?"

Ascham drew a long breath; then he said slowly: "Sit down, Granice. Let's talk."

II

Granice told his story simply, connectedly.

He began by a quick survey of his early years, the years of drudgery and privation. His father, a charming man who could never say "no," had so signally failed to say it on certain essential occasions that when he died he left an illegitimate family and a mortgaged estate. His lawful kin found themselves hanging over a gulf of debt, and young Granice, to support his mother and sister, had to leave Harvard and bury himself at eighteen in a broker's office. He loathed his work, and he was always poor, always worried and in ill-health. A few years later his mother died, but his sister, an ineffectual neurasthenic, remained on his hands. His own health gave out, and he had to go away for six months, and work harder than ever when he came back. He had no knack for business, no head for figures, no dimmest insight into the mysteries of commerce. He wanted to travel and write, those were his inmost longings. And as the years dragged on, and he neared middle-age without making any more money, or acquiring any firmer health, a sick despair possessed him. He tried writing, but he always came home from the office so tired that his brain could not work. For half the year he did not reach his dim up-town flat till after dark, and could only "brush up" for dinner, and afterward lie on the lounge with his pipe, while his sister droned through the evening paper. Sometimes he spent an evening at the theatre; or he dined out, or, more rarely, strayed off with an acquaintance or two in quest of what is known as "pleasure." And in summer, when he and Kate went to the sea-side for a month, he dozed through the days in utter weariness. Once he fell in love with a charming girl but what had he to offer her, in God's name? She seemed to like him, and in common decency he had to drop out of the running. Apparently no one replaced him, for she never married, but grew stoutish, grayish, philanthropic, yet how sweet she had been when he had first kissed her! One more wasted life, he reflected. . .

But the stage had always been his master-passion. He would have sold his soul for the time and freedom to write plays! It was in him, he could not remember when it had not been his deepest-seated instinct. As the years passed it became a morbid, a relentless obsession, yet with every year the material conditions were more and more against it. He felt himself growing middle-aged, and he watched the reflection of the process in his sister's wasted face. At eighteen she had been pretty, and as full of enthusiasm as he. Now she was sour, trivial, insignificant, she had missed her chance of life. And she had no resources, poor creature, was fashioned simply for the primitive functions she had been denied the chance to fulfil! It exasperated him to think of it and to reflect that even now a little travel, a little health, a little money, might transform her, make her young and desirable. . . The chief fruit of his experience was that there is no such fixed state as age or youth-there is only health as against sickness, wealth as against poverty; and age or youth as the outcome of the lot one draws.

At this point in his narrative Granice stood up, and went to lean against the mantel-piece, looking down at Ascham, who had not moved from his seat, or changed his attitude of rigid fascinated attention.

"Then came the summer when we went to Wrenfield to be near old Lenman, my mother's cousin, as you know. Some of the family always mounted guard over him, generally a niece or so. But that year they were all scattered, and one of the nieces offered to lend us her cottage if we'd relieve her of duty for two months. It was a nuisance for me, of course, for Wrenfield is two hours from town; but my mother, who was a slave to family observances, had always been good to the old man, so it was natural we should be called on and there was the saving of rent and the good air for Kate. So we went.

"You never knew Joseph Lenman? Well, picture to yourself an amoeba or some primitive organism of that sort, under a Titan's microscope. He was large, undifferentiated, inert, since I could remember him he had done nothing but take his temperature and read the Churchman. Oh, and cultivate melons, that was his hobby. Not vulgar, out-of-door melons, his were grown under glass. He had miles of it at Wrenfield, his big kitchen-garden was surrounded by blinking battalions of green-houses. And in nearly all of them melons were grown, early melons and late, French, English, domestic, dwarf melons and monsters: every shape, colour and variety. They were petted and nursed like children, a staff of trained attendants waited on them. I'm not sure they didn't have a doctor to take their temperature, at any rate the place was full of thermometers. And they didn't sprawl on the ground like ordinary melons; they were trained against the glass like nectarines, and each melon hung in a net which sustained its weight and left it free on all sides to the sun and air. . .

"It used to strike me sometimes that old Lenman was just like one of his own melons, the pale-fleshed English kind. His life, apathetic and motionless, hung in a net of gold, in an equable warm ventilated atmosphere, high above sordid earthly worries. The cardinal rule of his existence was not to let himself be 'worried.' . . . I remember his advising me to try it myself, one day when I spoke to him about Kate's bad health, and her need of a change. 'I never let myself worry,' he said complacently. 'It's the worst thing for the liver and you look to me as if you had a liver. Take my advice and be cheerful. You'll make yourself happier and others too.' And all he had to do was to write a cheque, and send the poor girl off for a holiday!

"The hardest part of it was that the money half-belonged to us already. The old skin-flint only had it for life, in trust for us and the others. But his life was a good deal sounder than mine or Kate's and one could picture him taking extra care of it for the joke of keeping us waiting. I always felt that the sight of our hungry eyes was a tonic to him.

"Well, I tried to see if I couldn't reach him through his vanity. I flattered him, feigned a passionate interest in his melons. And he was taken in, and used to discourse on them by the hour. On fine days he was driven to the green-houses in his pony-chair, and waddled through them, prodding and leering at the fruit, like a fat Turk in his seraglio. When he bragged to me of the expense of growing them I was reminded of a hideous old Lothario bragging of what his pleasures cost. And the resemblance was completed by the fact that he couldn't eat as much as a mouthful of his melons, had lived for years on buttermilk and toast. 'But, after all, it's my only hobby, why shouldn't I indulge it?' he said sentimentally. As if I'd ever been able to indulge any of mine! On the keep of those melons Kate and I could have lived like gods. . .

"One day toward the end of the summer, when Kate was too unwell to drag herself up to the big house, she asked me to go and spend the afternoon with cousin Joseph. It was a lovely soft September afternoon, a day to lie under a Roman stone-pine, with one's eyes on the sky, and let the cosmic harmonies rush through one. Perhaps the vision was suggested by the fact that, as I entered cousin Joseph's hideous black walnut library, I passed one of the under-gardeners, a handsome full-throated Italian, who dashed out in such a hurry that he nearly knocked me down. I remember thinking it queer that the fellow, whom I had often seen about the melon-houses, did not bow to me, or even seem to see me.

"Cousin Joseph sat in his usual seat, behind the darkened windows, his fat hands folded on his protuberant waistcoat, the last number of the Churchman at his elbow, and near it, on a huge dish, a fat melon, the fattest melon I'd ever seen. As I looked at it I pictured the ecstasy of contemplation from which I must have roused him, and congratulated myself on finding him in such a mood, since I had made up my mind to ask him a favour. Then I noticed that his face, instead of looking as calm as an eggshell, was distorted and whimpering and without stopping to greet me he pointed passionately to the melon.

"'Look at it, look at it, did you ever see such a beauty? Such firmness, roundness, such delicious smoothness to the touch?' It was as if he had said 'she' instead of 'it,' and when he put out his senile hand and touched the melon I positively had to look the other way.

"Then he told me what had happened. The Italian under-gardener, who had been specially recommended for the melon-houses, though it was against my cousin's principles to employ a Papist, had been assigned to the care of the monster: for it had revealed itself, early in its existence, as destined to become a monster, to surpass its plumpest, pulpiest sisters, carry off prizes at agricultural shows, and be photographed and celebrated in every gardening paper in the land. The Italian had done well, seemed to have a sense of responsibility. And that very morning he had been ordered to pick the melon, which was to be shown next day at the county fair, and to bring it in for Mr. Lenman to gaze on its blonde virginity. But in picking it, what had the damned scoundrelly Jesuit done but drop it, drop it crash on the sharp spout of a watering-pot, so that it received a deep gash in its firm pale rotundity, and was henceforth but a bruised, ruined, fallen melon?

"The old man's rage was fearful in its impotence, he shook, spluttered and strangled with it. He had just had the Italian up and had sacked him on the spot, without wages or character, had threatened to have him arrested if he was ever caught prowling about Wrenfield. 'By God, and I'll do it, I'll write to Washington, I'll have the pauper scoundrel deported! I'll show him what money can do!' As likely as not there was some murderous Black-hand business under it, it would be found that the fellow was a member of a 'gang.' Those Italians would murder you for a quarter. He meant to have the police look into it. . . And then he grew frightened at his own excitement. 'But I must calm myself,' he said. He took his temperature, rang for his drops, and turned to the Churchman. He had been reading an article on Nestorianism when the melon was brought in. He asked me to go on with it, and I read to him for an hour, in the dim close room, with a fat fly buzzing stealthily about the fallen melon.

"All the while one phrase of the old man's buzzed in my brain like the fly about the melon. 'I'll show him what money can do!' Good heaven! If I could but show the old man! If I could make him see his power of giving happiness as a new outlet for his monstrous egotism! I tried to tell him something about my situation and Kate's, spoke of my ill-health, my unsuccessful drudgery, my longing to write, to make myself a name, I stammered out an entreaty for a loan. 'I can guarantee to repay you, sir-I've a half-written play as security. . .'

"I shall never forget his glassy stare. His face had grown as smooth as an egg-shell again, his eyes peered over his fat cheeks like sentinels over a slippery rampart.

"'A half-written play, a play of yours as security?' He looked at me almost fearfully, as if detecting the first symptoms of insanity. 'Do you understand anything of business?' he enquired mildly. I laughed and answered: 'No, not much.'

"He leaned back with closed lids. 'All this excitement has been too much for me,' he said. 'If you'll excuse me, I'll prepare for my nap.' And I stumbled out of the room, blindly, like the Italian."

Granice moved away from the mantel-piece, and walked across to the tray set out with decanters and soda-water. He poured himself a tall glass of soda-water, emptied it, and glanced at Ascham's dead cigar.

"Better light another," he suggested.

The lawyer shook his head, and Granice went on with his tale. He told of his mounting obsession, how the murderous impulse had waked in him on the instant of his cousin's refusal, and he had muttered to himself: "By God, if you won't, I'll make you." He spoke more tranquilly as the narrative proceeded, as though his rage had died down once the resolve to act on it was taken. He applied his whole mind to the question of how the old man was to be "disposed of." Suddenly he remembered the outcry: "Those Italians will murder you for a quarter!" But no definite project presented itself: he simply waited for an inspiration.

Granice and his sister moved to town a day or two after the incident of the melon. But the cousins, who had returned, kept them informed of the old man's condition. One day, about three weeks later, Granice, on getting home, found Kate excited over a report from Wrenfield. The Italian had been there again, had somehow slipped into the house, made his way up to the library, and "used threatening language." The house-keeper found cousin Joseph gasping, the whites of his eyes showing "something awful." The doctor was sent for, and the attack warded off; and the police had ordered the Italian from the neighbourhood.

But cousin Joseph, thereafter, languished, had "nerves," and lost his taste for toast and butter-milk. The doctor called in a colleague, and the consultation amused and excited the old man-he became once more an important figure. The medical men reassured the family too completely! and to the patient they recommended a more varied diet: advised him to take whatever "tempted him." And so one day, tremulously, prayerfully, he decided on a tiny bit of melon. It was brought up with ceremony, and consumed in the presence of the house-keeper and a hovering cousin; and twenty minutes later he was dead. . .

"But you remember the circumstances," Granice went on; "how suspicion turned at once on the Italian? In spite of the hint the police had given him he had been seen hanging about the house since 'the scene.' It was said that he had tender relations with the kitchen-maid, and the rest seemed easy to explain. But when they looked round to ask him for the explanation he was gone, gone clean out of sight. He had been 'warned' to leave Wrenfield, and he had taken the warning so to heart that no one ever laid eyes on him again."

Granice paused. He had dropped into a chair opposite the lawyer's, and he sat for a moment, his head thrown back, looking about the familiar room. Everything in it had grown grimacing and alien, and each strange insistent object seemed craning forward from its place to hear him.

"It was I who put the stuff in the melon," he said. "And I don't want you to think I'm sorry for it. This isn't 'remorse,' understand. I'm glad the old skin-flint is dead, I'm glad the others have their money. But mine's no use to me any more. My sister married miserably, and died. And I've never had what I wanted."

Ascham continued to stare; then he said: "What on earth was your object, then?"

"Why, to get what I wanted, what I fancied was in reach! I wanted change, rest, life, for both of us, wanted, above all, for myself, the chance to write! I travelled, got back my health, and came home to tie myself up to my work. And I've slaved at it steadily for ten years without reward, without the most distant hope of success! Nobody will look at my stuff. And now I'm fifty, and I'm beaten, and I know it." His chin dropped forward on his breast. "I want to chuck the whole business," he ended.

III

It was after midnight when Ascham left.

His hand on Granice's shoulder, as he turned to go "District Attorney be hanged; see a doctor, see a doctor!" he had cried; and so, with an exaggerated laugh, had pulled on his coat and departed.

Granice turned back into the library. It had never occurred to him that Ascham would not believe his story. For three hours he had explained, elucidated, patiently and painfully gone over every detail but without once breaking down the iron incredulity of the lawyer's eye.

At first Ascham had feigned to be convinced but that, as Granice now perceived, was simply to get him to expose himself, to entrap him into contradictions. And when the attempt failed, when Granice triumphantly met and refuted each disconcerting question, the lawyer dropped the mask suddenly, and said with a goodhumoured laugh: "By Jove, Granice you'll write a successful play yet. The way you've worked this all out is a marvel."

Granice swung about furiously, that last sneer about the play inflamed him. Was all the world in a conspiracy to deride his failure?

"I did it, I did it," he muttered sullenly, his rage spending itself against the impenetrable surface of the other's mockery; and Ascham answered with a smile: "Ever read any of those books on hallucination? I've got a fairly good medico-legal library. I could send you one or two if you like. . ."

Left alone, Granice cowered down in the chair before his writingtable. He understood that Ascham thought him off his head.

"Good God, what if they all think me crazy?"

The horror of it broke out over him in a cold sweat, he sat there and shook, his eyes hidden in his icy hands. But gradually, as he began to rehearse his story for the thousandth time, he saw again how incontrovertible it was, and felt sure that any criminal lawyer would believe him.

"That's the trouble, Ascham's not a criminal lawyer. And then he's a friend. What a fool I was to talk to a friend! Even if he did believe me, he'd never let me see it, his instinct would be to cover the whole thing up. . . But in that case, if he did believe me, he might think it a kindness to get me shut up in an asylum. . ." Granice began to tremble again. "Good heaven! If he should bring in an expert, one of those damned alienists! Ascham and Pettilow can do anything, their word always goes. If Ascham drops a hint that I'd better be shut up, I'll be in a strait-jacket by to-morrow! And he'd do it from the kindest motives, be quite right to do it if he thinks I'm a murderer!"

The vision froze him to his chair. He pressed his fists to his bursting temples and tried to think. For the first time he hoped that Ascham had not believed his story.

"But he did, he did! I can see it now, I noticed what a queer eye he cocked at me. Good God, what shall I do, what shall I do?"

He started up and looked at the clock. Half-past one. What if Ascham should think the case urgent, rout out an alienist, and come back with him? Granice jumped to his feet, and his sudden gesture brushed the morning paper from the table. Mechanically he stooped to pick it up, and the movement started a new train of association.

He sat down again, and reached for the telephone book in the rack by his chair.

"Give me three-o-ten . . . yes."

The new idea in his mind had revived his flagging energy. He would act, act at once. It was only by thus planning ahead, committing himself to some unavoidable line of conduct, that he could pull himself through the meaningless days. Each time he reached a fresh decision it was like coming out of a foggy weltering sea into a calm harbour with lights. One of the queerest phases of his long agony was the intense relief produced by these momentary lulls.

"That the office of the Investigator? Yes? Give me Mr. Denver, please. . . Hallo, Denver. . . Yes, Hubert Granice. . . . Just caught you? Going straight home? Can I come and see you . . . yes, now . . . have a talk? It's rather urgent . . . yes, might give you some first-rate 'copy.' . . . All right!" He hung up the receiver with a laugh. It had been a happy thought to call up the editor of the Investigator, Robert Denver was the very man he needed. . .

Granice put out the lights in the library, it was odd how the automatic gestures persisted! went into the hall, put on his hat and overcoat, and let himself out of the flat. In the hall, a sleepy elevator boy blinked at him and then dropped his head on his folded arms. Granice passed out into the street. At the corner of Fifth Avenue he hailed a crawling cab, and called out an up-town address. The long thoroughfare stretched before him, dim and deserted, like an ancient avenue of tombs. But from Denver's house a friendly beam fell on the pavement; and as Granice sprang from his cab the editor's electric turned the corner.

The two men grasped hands, and Denver, feeling for his latch-key, ushered Granice into the brightly-lit hall.

"Disturb me? Not a bit. You might have, at ten to-morrow morning . . . but this is my liveliest hour . . . you know my habits of old."

Granice had known Robert Denver for fifteen years, watched his rise through all the stages of journalism to the Olympian pinnacle of the Investigator's editorial office. In the thickset man with grizzling hair there were few traces left of the hungry-eyed young reporter who, on his way home in the small hours, used to "bob in" on Granice, while the latter sat grinding at his plays. Denver had to pass Granice's flat on the way to his own, and it became a habit, if he saw a light in the window, and Granice's shadow against the blind, to go in, smoke a pipe, and discuss the universe.

"Well, this is like old times, a good old habit reversed." The editor smote his visitor genially on the shoulder. "Reminds me of the nights when I used to rout you out. . . How's the play, by the way? There is a play, I suppose? It's as safe to ask you that as to say to some men: 'How's the baby?'"

Denver laughed good-naturedly, and Granice thought how thick and heavy he had grown. It was evident, even to Granice's tortured nerves, that the words had not been uttered in malice, and the fact gave him a new measure of his insignificance. Denver did not even know that he had been a failure! The fact hurt more than Ascham's irony.

"Come in, come in." The editor led the way into a small cheerful room, where there were cigars and decanters. He pushed an armchair toward his visitor, and dropped into another with a comfortable groan.

"Now, then, help yourself. And let's hear all about it."

He beamed at Granice over his pipe-bowl, and the latter, lighting his cigar, said to himself: "Success makes men comfortable, but it makes them stupid."

Then he turned, and began: "Denver, I want to tell you"

The clock ticked rhythmically on the mantel-piece. The little room was gradually filled with drifting blue layers of smoke, and through them the editor's face came and went like the moon through a moving sky. Once the hour struck, then the rhythmical ticking began again. The atmosphere grew denser and heavier, and beads of perspiration began to roll from Granice's forehead.

"Do you mind if I open the window?"

"No. It is stuffy in here. Wait, I'll do it myself." Denver pushed down the upper sash, and returned to his chair. "Well, go on," he said, filling another pipe. His composure exasperated Granice.

"There's no use in my going on if you don't believe me."

The editor remained unmoved. "Who says I don't believe you? And how can I tell till you've finished?"

Granice went on, ashamed of his outburst. "It was simple enough, as you'll see. From the day the old man said to me, 'Those Italians would murder you for a quarter,' I dropped everything and just worked at my scheme. It struck me at once that I must find a way of getting to Wrenfield and back in a night, and that led to the idea of a motor. A motor, that never occurred to you? You wonder where I got the money, I suppose. Well, I had a thousand or so put by, and I nosed around till I found what I wanted, a second-hand racer. I knew how to drive a car, and I tried the thing and found it was all right. Times were bad, and I bought it for my price, and stored it away. Where? Why, in one of those no-questions-asked garages where they keep motors that are not for family use. I had a lively cousin who had put me up to that dodge, and I looked about till I found a queer hole where they took in my car like a baby in a foundling asylum. . . Then I practiced running to Wrenfield and back in a night. I knew the way pretty well, for I'd done it often with the same lively cousin, and in the small hours, too. The distance is over ninety miles, and on the third trial I did it under two hours. But my arms were so lame that I could hardly get dressed the next morning. . .

"Well, then came the report about the Italian's threats, and I saw I must act at once. . . I meant to break into the old man's room, shoot him, and get away again. It was a big risk, but I thought I could manage it. Then we heard that he was ill, that there'd been a consultation. Perhaps the fates were going to do it for me! Good Lord, if that could only be! . . ."

Granice stopped and wiped his forehead: the open window did not seem to have cooled the room.

"Then came word that he was better; and the day after, when I came up from my office, I found Kate laughing over the news that he was to try a bit of melon. The house-keeper had just telephoned her, all Wrenfield was in a flutter. The doctor himself had picked out the melon, one of the little French ones that are hardly bigger than a large tomato, and the patient was to eat it at his breakfast the next morning.

"In a flash I saw my chance. It was a bare chance, no more. But I knew the ways of the house, I was sure the melon would be brought in over night and put in the pantry ice-box. If there were only one melon in the ice-box I could be fairly sure it was the one I wanted. Melons didn't lie around loose in that house- every one was known, numbered, catalogued. The old man was beset by the dread that the servants would eat them, and he took a hundred mean precautions to prevent it. Yes, I felt pretty sure of my melon . . . and poisoning was much safer than shooting. It would have been the devil and all to get into the old man's bedroom without his rousing the house; but I ought to be able to break into the pantry without much trouble.

"It was a cloudy night, too, everything served me. I dined quietly, and sat down at my desk. Kate had one of her usual headaches, and went to bed early. As soon as she was gone I slipped out. I had got together a sort of disguise, red beard and queer-looking ulster. I shoved them into a bag, and went round to the garage. There was no one there but a half-drunken machinist whom I'd never seen before. That served me, too. They were always changing machinists, and this new fellow didn't even bother to ask if the car belonged to me. It was a very easygoing place. . .

"Well, I jumped in, ran up Broadway, and let the car go as soon as I was out of Harlem. Dark as it was, I could trust myself to strike a sharp pace. In the shadow of a wood I stopped a second and got into the beard and ulster. Then away again, it was just eleven-thirty when I got to Wrenfield.

"I left the car in a dark lane behind the Lenman place, and slipped through the kitchen-garden. The melon-houses winked at me through the dark, I remember thinking that they knew what I wanted to know. . . . By the stable a dog came out growling, but he nosed me out, jumped on me, and went back. . . The house was as dark as the grave. I knew everybody went to bed by ten. But there might be a prowling servant, the kitchen-maid might have come down to let in her Italian. I had to risk that, of course. I crept around by the back door and hid in the shrubbery. Then I listened. It was all as silent as death. I crossed over to the house, pried open the pantry window and climbed in. I had a little electric lamp in my pocket, and shielding it with my cap I groped my way to the ice-box, opened it, and there was the little French melon . . . only one.

"I stopped to listen, I was quite cool. Then I pulled out my bottle of stuff and my syringe, and gave each section of the melon a hypodermic. It was all done inside of three minutes, at ten minutes to twelve I was back in the car. I got out of the lane as quietly as I could, struck a back road that skirted the village, and let the car out as soon as I was beyond the last houses. I only stopped once on the way in, to drop the beard and ulster into a pond. I had a big stone ready to weight them with and they went down plump, like a dead body, and at two o'clock I was back at my desk."

Granice stopped speaking and looked across the smoke-fumes at his listener; but Denver's face remained inscrutable.

At length he said: "Why did you want to tell me this?"

The question startled Granice. He was about to explain, as he had explained to Ascham; but suddenly it occurred to him that if his motive had not seemed convincing to the lawyer it would carry much less weight with Denver. Both were successful men, and success does not understand the subtle agony of failure. Granice cast about for another reason.

"Why, I, the thing haunts me . . . remorse, I suppose you'd call it. . ."

Denver struck the ashes from his empty pipe.

"Remorse? Bosh!" he said energetically.

Granice's heart sank. "You don't believe in remorse?"

"Not an atom: in the man of action. The mere fact of your talking of remorse proves to me that you're not the man to have planned and put through such a job."

Granice groaned. "Well, I lied to you about remorse. I've never felt any."

Denver's lips tightened sceptically about his freshly-filled pipe. "What was your motive, then? You must have had one."

"I'll tell you" And Granice began again to rehearse the story of his failure, of his loathing for life. "Don't say you don't believe me this time . . . that this isn't a real reason!" he stammered out piteously as he ended.

Denver meditated. "No, I won't say that. I've seen too many queer things. There's always a reason for wanting to get out of life, the wonder is that we find so many for staying in!" Granice's heart grew light. "Then you do believe me?" he faltered.

"Believe that you're sick of the job? Yes. And that you haven't the nerve to pull the trigger? Oh, yes, that's easy enough, too. But all that doesn't make you a murderer, though I don't say it proves you could never have been one."

"I have been one, Denver, I swear to you."

"Perhaps." He meditated. "Just tell me one or two things."

"Oh, go ahead. You won't stump me!" Granice heard himself say with a laugh.

"Well, how did you make all those trial trips without exciting your sister's curiosity? I knew your night habits pretty well at that time, remember. You were very seldom out late. Didn't the change in your ways surprise her?"

"No; because she was away at the time. She went to pay several visits in the country soon after we came back from Wrenfield, and was only in town for a night or two before, before I did the job."

"And that night she went to bed early with a headache?"

"Yes, blinding. She didn't know anything when she had that kind. And her room was at the back of the flat."

Denver again meditated. "And when you got back, she didn't hear you? You got in without her knowing it?"

"Yes. I went straight to my work, took it up at the word where I'd left off. Why, Denver, don't you remember?" Granice suddenly, passionately interjected.

"Remember?"

"Yes; how you found me, when you looked in that morning, between two and three . . . your usual hour . . .?"

"Yes," the editor nodded.

Granice gave a short laugh. "In my old coat, with my pipe: looked as if I'd been working all night, didn't I? Well, I hadn't been in my chair ten minutes!"

Denver uncrossed his legs and then crossed them again. "I didn't know whether you remembered that."

"What?"

"My coming in that particular night or morning."

Granice swung round in his chair. "Why, man alive! That's why I'm here now. Because it was you who spoke for me at the inquest, when they looked round to see what all the old man's heirs had been doing that night, you who testified to having dropped in and found me at my desk as usual. . . . I thought that would appeal to your journalistic sense if nothing else would!"

Denver smiled. "Oh, my journalistic sense is still susceptible enough, and the idea's picturesque, I grant you: asking the man who proved your alibi to establish your guilt."

"That's it, that's it!" Granice's laugh had a ring of triumph.

"Well, but how about the other chap's testimony, I mean that young doctor: what was his name? Ned Ranney. Don't you remember my testifying that I'd met him at the elevated station, and told him I was on my way to smoke a pipe with you, and his saying: 'All right; you'll find him in. I passed the house two hours ago, and saw his shadow against the blind, as usual.' And the lady with the toothache in the flat across the way: she corroborated his statement, you remember."

"Yes; I remember."

Well, then?"

"Simple enough. Before starting I rigged up a kind of mannikin with old coats and a cushion, something to cast a shadow on the blind. All you fellows were used to seeing my shadow there in the small hours, I counted on that, and knew you'd take any vague outline as mine."

"Simple enough, as you say. But the woman with the toothache saw the shadow move, you remember she said she saw you sink forward, as if you'd fallen asleep."

"Yes; and she was right. It did move. I suppose some extra-heavy dray must have jolted by the flimsy building, at any rate, something gave my mannikin a jar, and when I came back he had sunk forward, half over the table."

There was a long silence between the two men. Granice, with a throbbing heart, watched Denver refill his pipe. The editor, at any rate, did not sneer and flout him. After all, journalism gave a deeper insight than the law into the fantastic possibilities of life, prepared one better to allow for the incalculableness of human impulses.

"Well?" Granice faltered out.

Denver stood up with a shrug. "Look here, man, what's wrong with you? Make a clean breast of it! Nerves gone to smash? I'd like to take you to see a chap I know, an ex-prize-fighter, who's a wonder at pulling fellows in your state out of their hole"

"Oh, oh" Granice broke in. He stood up also, and the two men eyed each other. "You don't believe me, then?"

"This yarn, how can I? There wasn't a flaw in your alibi."

"But haven't I filled it full of them now?"

Denver shook his head. "I might think so if I hadn't happened to know that you wanted to. There's the hitch, don't you see?"

Granice groaned. "No, I didn't. You mean my wanting to be found guilty?"

"Of course! If somebody else had accused you, the story might have been worth looking into. As it is, a child could have invented it. It doesn't do much credit to your ingenuity."

Granice turned sullenly toward the door. What was the use of arguing? But on the threshold a sudden impulse drew him back. "Look here, Denver, I daresay you're right. But will you do just one thing to prove it? Put my statement in the Investigator, just as I've made it. Ridicule it as much as you like. Only give the other fellows a chance at it, men who don't know anything about me. Set them talking and looking about. I don't care a damn whether you believe me, what I want is to convince the Grand Jury! I oughtn't to have come to a man who knows me-your cursed incredulity is infectious. I don't put my case well, because I know in advance it's discredited, and I almost end by not believing it myself. That's why I can't convince YOU. It's a vicious circle." He laid a hand on Denver's arm. "Send a stenographer, and put my statement in the paper.

But Denver did not warm to the idea. "My dear fellow, you seem to forget that all the evidence was pretty thoroughly sifted at the time, every possible clue followed up. The public would have been ready enough then to believe that you murdered old Lenman-you or anybody else. All they wanted was a murderer, the most improbable would have served. But your alibi was too confoundedly complete. And nothing you've told me has shaken it." Denver laid his cool hand over the other's burning fingers. "Look here, old fellow, go home and work up a better case, then come in and submit it to the Investigator."

IV

The perspiration was rolling off Granice's forehead. Every few minutes he had to draw out his handkerchief and wipe the moisture from his haggard face.

For an hour and a half he had been talking steadily, putting his case to the District Attorney. Luckily he had a speaking acquaintance with Allonby, and had obtained, without much difficulty, a private audience on the very day after his talk with Robert Denver. In the interval between he had hurried home, got out of his evening clothes, and gone forth again at once into the dreary dawn. His fear of Ascham and the alienist made it impossible for him to remain in his rooms. And it seemed to him that the only way of averting that hideous peril was by establishing, in some sane impartial mind, the proof of his guilt. Even if he had not been so incurably sick of life, the electric chair seemed now the only alternative to the straitjacket.

As he paused to wipe his forehead he saw the District Attorney glance at his watch. The gesture was significant, and Granice lifted an appealing hand. "I don't expect you to believe me now-but can't you put me under arrest, and have the thing looked into?"

Allonby smiled faintly under his heavy grayish moustache. He had a ruddy face, full and jovial, in which his keen professional eyes seemed to keep watch over impulses not strictly professional.

"Well, I don't know that we need lock you up just yet. But of course I'm bound to look into your statement"

Granice rose with an exquisite sense of relief. Surely Allonby wouldn't have said that if he hadn't believed him!

"That's all right. Then I needn't detain you. I can be found at any time at my apartment." He gave the address.

The District Attorney smiled again, more openly. "What do you say to leaving it for an hour or two this evening? I'm giving a little supper at Rector's, quiet, little affair, you understand: just Miss Melrose, I think you know her, and a friend or two; and if you'll join us. . ."

Granice stumbled out of the office without knowing what reply he had made.

He waited for four days, four days of concentrated horror. During the first twenty-four hours the fear of Ascham's alienist dogged him; and as that subsided, it was replaced by the exasperating sense that his avowal had made no impression on the District Attorney. Evidently, if he had been going to look into the case, Allonby would have been heard from before now. . . . And that mocking invitation to supper showed clearly enough how little the story had impressed him!

Granice was overcome by the futility of any farther attempt to inculpate himself. He was chained to life, a "prisoner of consciousness." Where was it he had read the phrase? Well, he was learning what it meant. In the glaring night-hours, when his brain seemed ablaze, he was visited by a sense of his fixed identity, of his irreducible, inexpugnable selfness , keener, more insidious, more unescapable, than any sensation he had ever known. He had not guessed that the mind was capable of such intricacies of self-realization, of penetrating so deep into its own dark windings. Often he woke from his brief snatches of sleep with the feeling that something material was clinging to him, was on his hands and face, and in his throat, and as his brain cleared he understood that it was the sense of his own loathed personality that stuck to him like some thick viscous substance.

Then, in the first morning hours, he would rise and look out of his window at the awakening activities of the street, at the street-cleaners, the ash-cart drivers, and the other dingy workers flitting hurriedly by through the sallow winter light. Oh, to be one of them, any of them, to take his chance in any of their skins! They were the toilers, the men whose lot was pitied, the victims wept over and ranted about by altruists and economists; and how gladly he would have taken up the load of any one of them, if only he might have shaken off his own! But, no-the iron circle of consciousness held them too: each one was hand-cuffed to his own hideous ego. Why wish to be any one man rather than another? The only absolute good was not to be . . . And Flint, coming in to draw his bath, would ask if he preferred his eggs scrambled or poached that morning?

On the fifth day he wrote a long urgent letter to Allonby; and for the succeeding two days he had the occupation of waiting for an answer. He hardly stirred from his rooms, in his fear of missing the letter by a moment; but would the District Attorney write, or send a representative: a policeman, a "secret agent," or some other mysterious emissary of the law?

On the third morning Flint, stepping softly, as if, confound it! his master were ill, entered the library where Granice sat behind an unread newspaper, and proferred a card on a tray.

Granice read the name, J. B. Hewson, and underneath, in pencil, "From the District Attorney's office." He started up with a thumping heart, and signed an assent to the servant.

Mr. Hewson was a slight sallow nondescript man of about fifty-the kind of man of whom one is sure to see a specimen in any crowd. "Just the type of the successful detective," Granice reflected as he shook hands with his visitor.

And it was in that character that Mr. Hewson briefly introduced himself. He had been sent by the District Attorney to have "a quiet talk" with Mr. Granice, to ask him to repeat the statement he had made about the Lenman murder.

His manner was so quiet, so reasonable and receptive, that Granice's self-confidence returned. Here was a sensible man, a man who knew his business, it would be easy enough to make him see through that ridiculous alibi! Granice offered Mr. Hewson a cigar, and lighting one himself, to prove his coolness, began again to tell his story.

He was conscious, as he proceeded, of telling it better than ever before. Practice helped, no doubt; and his listener's detached, impartial attitude helped still more. He could see that Hewson, at least, had not decided in advance to disbelieve him, and the sense of being trusted made him more lucid and more consecutive. Yes, this time his words would certainly carry conviction. . .

V

Despairingly, Granice gazed up and down the shabby street. Beside him stood a young man with bright prominent eyes, a smooth but not too smoothly-shaven face, and an Irish smile. The young man's nimble glance followed Granice's.

"Sure of the number, are you?" he asked briskly.

"Oh, yes, it was 104."

"Well, then, the new building has swallowed it up, that's certain."

He tilted his head back and surveyed the half-finished front of a brick and limestone flat-house that reared its flimsy elegance above a row of tottering tenements and stables.

"Dead sure?" he repeated.

"Yes," said Granice, discouraged. "And even if I hadn't been, I know the garage was just opposite Leffler's over there." He pointed across the street to a tumble-down stable with a blotched sign on which the words "Livery and Boarding" were still faintly discernible.

The young man dashed across to the opposite pavement. "Well, that's something, may get a clue there. Leffler's, same name there, anyhow. You remember that name?"

"Yes, distinctly."

Granice had felt a return of confidence since he had enlisted the interest of the Explorer's "smartest" reporter. If there were moments when he hardly believed his own story, there were others when it seemed impossible that every one should not believe it; and young Peter McCarren, peering, listening, questioning, jotting down notes, inspired him with an exquisite sense of security. McCarren had fastened on the case at once, "like a leech," as he phrased it, jumped at it, thrilled to it, and settled down to "draw the last drop of fact from it, and had not let go till he had." No one else had treated Granice in that way, even Allonby's detective had not taken a single note. And though a week had elapsed since the visit of that authorized official, nothing had been heard from the District Attorney's office: Allonby had apparently dropped the matter again. But McCarren wasn't going to drop it, not he! He positively hung on Granice's footsteps. They had spent the greater part of the previous day together, and now they were off again, running down clues.

But at Leffler's they got none, after all. Leffler's was no longer a stable. It was condemned to demolition, and in the respite between sentence and execution it had become a vague place of storage, a hospital for broken-down carriages and carts, presided over by a blear-eyed old woman who knew nothing of Flood's garage across the way, did not even remember what had stood there before the new flat-house began to rise.

"Well, we may run Leffler down somewhere; I've seen harder jobs done," said McCarren, cheerfully noting down the name.

As they walked back toward Sixth Avenue he added, in a less sanguine tone: "I'd undertake now to put the thing through if you could only put me on the track of that cyanide."

Granice's heart sank. Yes, there was the weak spot; he had felt it from the first! But he still hoped to convince McCarren that his case was strong enough without it; and he urged the reporter to come back to his rooms and sum up the facts with him again.

"Sorry, Mr. Granice, but I'm due at the office now. Besides, it'd be no use till I get some fresh stuff to work on. Suppose I call you up tomorrow or next day?"

He plunged into a trolley and left Granice gazing desolately after him.

Two days later he reappeared at the apartment, a shade less jaunty in demeanor.

"Well, Mr. Granice, the stars in their courses are against you, as the bard says. Can't get a trace of Flood, or of Leffler either. And you say you bought the motor through Flood, and sold it through him, too?"

"Yes," said Granice wearily.

"Who bought it, do you know?"

Granice wrinkled his brows. "Why, Flood, yes, Flood himself. I sold it back to him three months later."

"Flood? The devil! And I've ransacked the town for Flood. That kind of business disappears as if the earth had swallowed it."

Granice, discouraged, kept silence.

"That brings us back to the poison," McCarren continued, his note-book out. "Just go over that again, will you?"

And Granice went over it again. It had all been so simple at the time, and he had been so clever in covering up his traces! As soon as he decided on poison he looked about for an acquaintance who manufactured chemicals; and there was Jim Dawes, a Harvard classmate, in the dyeing business, just the man. But at the last moment it occurred to him that suspicion might turn toward so obvious an opportunity, and he decided on a more tortuous course. Another friend, Carrick Venn, a student of medicine whom irremediable ill-health had kept from the practice of his profession, amused his leisure with experiments in physics, for the exercise of which he had set up a simple laboratory. Granice had the habit of dropping in to smoke a cigar with him on Sunday afternoons, and the friends generally sat in Venn's work-shop, at the back of the old family house in Stuyvesant Square. Off this work-shop was the cupboard of supplies, with its row of deadly bottles. Carrick Venn was an original, a man of restless curious tastes, and his place, on a Sunday, was often full of visitors: a cheerful crowd of journalists, scribblers, painters, experimenters in divers forms of expression. Coming and going among so many, it was easy enough to pass unperceived; and one afternoon Granice, arriving before Venn had returned home, found himself alone in the work-shop, and quickly slipping into the cupboard, transferred the drug to his pocket.

But that had happened ten years ago; and Venn, poor fellow, was long since dead of his dragging ailment. His old father was dead, too, the house in Stuyvesant Square had been turned into a boarding-house, and the shifting life of New York had passed its rapid sponge over every trace of their obscure little history. Even the optimistic McCarren seemed to acknowledge the hopelessness of seeking for proof in that direction.

"And there's the third door slammed in our faces." He shut his note-book, and throwing back his head, rested his bright inquisitive eyes on Granice's furrowed face.

"Look here, Mr. Granice, you see the weak spot, don't you?"

The other made a despairing motion. "I see so many!"

"Yes: but the one that weakens all the others. Why the deuce do you want this thing known? Why do you want to put your head into the noose?"

Granice looked at him hopelessly, trying to take the measure of his quick light irreverent mind. No one so full of a cheerful animal life would believe in the craving for death as a sufficient motive; and Granice racked his brain for one more convincing. But suddenly he saw the reporter's face soften, and melt to a naive sentimentalism.

"Mr. Granice, has the memory of it always haunted you?"

Granice stared a moment, and then leapt at the opening. "That's it, the memory of it . . . always . . ."

McCarren nodded vehemently. "Dogged your steps, eh? Wouldn't let you sleep? The time came when you had to make a clean breast of it?"

"I had to. Can't you understand?"

The reporter struck his fist on the table. "God, sir! I don't suppose there's a human being with a drop of warm blood in him that can't picture the deadly horrors of remorse"

The Celtic imagination was aflame, and Granice mutely thanked him for the word. What neither Ascham nor Denver would accept as a conceivable motive the Irish reporter seized on as the most adequate; and, as he said, once one could find a convincing motive, the difficulties of the case became so many incentives to effort.

"Remorse, REMORSE," he repeated, rolling the word under his tongue with an accent that was a clue to the psychology of the popular drama; and Granice, perversely, said to himself: "If I could only have struck that note I should have been running in six theatres at once."

He saw that from that moment McCarren's professional zeal would be fanned by emotional curiosity; and he profited by the fact to propose that they should dine together, and go on afterward to some music-hall or theatre. It was becoming necessary to Granice to feel himself an object of pre-occupation, to find himself in another mind. He took a kind of gray penumbral pleasure in riveting McCarren's attention on his case; and to feign the grimaces of moral anguish became a passionately engrossing game. He had not entered a theatre for months; but he sat out the meaningless performance in rigid tolerance, sustained by the sense of the reporter's observation.

Between the acts, McCarren amused him with anecdotes about the audience: he knew every one by sight, and could lift the curtain from every physiognomy. Granice listened indulgently. He had lost all interest in his kind, but he knew that he was himself the real centre of McCarren's attention, and that every word the latter spoke had an indirect bearing on his own problem.

"See that fellow over there, the little dried-up man in the third row, pulling his moustache? His memoirs would be worth publishing," McCarren said suddenly in the last entr'acte.

Granice, following his glance, recognized the detective from Allonby's office. For a moment he had the thrilling sense that he was being shadowed.

"Caesar, if he could talk!" McCarren continued. "Know who he is, of course? Dr. John B. Stell, the biggest alienist in the country"

Granice, with a start, bent again between the heads in front of him. "That man, the fourth from the aisle? You're mistaken. That's not Dr. Stell."

McCarren laughed. "Well, I guess I've been in court enough to know Stell when I see him. He testifies in nearly all the big cases where they plead insanity."

A cold shiver ran down Granice's spine, but he repeated obstinately: "That's not Dr. Stell."

"Not Stell? Why, man, I know him. Look, here he comes. If it isn't Stell, he won't speak to me."

The little dried-up man was moving slowly up the aisle. As he neared McCarren he made a slight gesture of recognition.

"How'do, Doctor Stell? Pretty slim show, ain't it?" the reporter cheerfully flung out at him. And Mr. J. B. Hewson, with a nod of amicable assent, passed on.

Granice sat benumbed. He knew he had not been mistaken, the man who had just passed was the same man whom Allonby had sent to see him: a physician disguised as a detective. Allonby, then, had thought him insane, like the others, had regarded his confession as the maundering of a maniac. The discovery froze Granice with horror, he seemed to see the mad-house gaping for him.

"Isn't there a man a good deal like him, a detective named J. B. Hewson?"

But he knew in advance what McCarren's answer would be. "Hewson? J. B. Hewson? Never heard of him. But that was J. B. Stell fast enough, I guess he can be trusted to know himself, and you saw he answered to his name."

VI

Some days passed before Granice could obtain a word with the District Attorney: he began to think that Allonby avoided him.
But when they were face to face Allonby's jovial countenance showed no sign of embarrassment. He waved his visitor to a chair, and leaned across his desk with the encouraging smile of a consulting physician.

Granice broke out at once: "That detective you sent me the other day"

Allonby raised a deprecating hand.

"I know: it was Stell the alienist. Why did you do that, Allonby?"

The other's face did not lose its composure. "Because I looked up your story first and there's nothing in it."

"Nothing in it?" Granice furiously interposed.

"Absolutely nothing. If there is, why the deuce don't you bring me proofs? I know you've been talking to Peter Ascham, and to Denver, and to that little ferret McCarren of the Explorer. Have any of them been able to make out a case for you? No. Well, what am I to do?"

Granice's lips began to tremble. "Why did you play me that trick?"

"About Stell? I had to, my dear fellow: it's part of my business. Stell is a detective, if you come to that, every doctor is."

The trembling of Granice's lips increased, communicating itself in a long quiver to his facial muscles. He forced a laugh through his dry throat. "Well, and what did he detect?"

"In you? Oh, he thinks it's overwork, overwork and too much smoking. If you look in on him some day at his office he'll show you the record of hundreds of cases like yours, and advise you what treatment to follow. It's one of the commonest forms of hallucination. Have a cigar, all the same."

"But, Allonby, I killed that man!"

The District Attorney's large hand, outstretched on his desk, had an almost imperceptible gesture, and a moment later, as if an answer to the call of an electric bell, a clerk looked in from the outer office.

"Sorry, my dear fellow, lot of people waiting. Drop in on Stell some morning," Allonby said, shaking hands.

McCarren had to own himself beaten: there was absolutely no flaw in the alibi. And since his duty to his journal obviously forbade his wasting time on insoluble mysteries, he ceased to frequent Granice, who dropped back into a deeper isolation. For a day or two after his visit to Allonby he continued to live in dread of Dr. Stell. Why might not Allonby have deceived him as to the alienist's diagnosis? What if he were really being shadowed, not by a police agent but by a mad-doctor? To have the truth out, he suddenly determined to call on Dr. Stell.

The physician received him kindly, and reverted without embarrassment to the conditions of their previous meeting. "We have to do that occasionally, Mr. Granice; it's one of our methods. And you had given Allonby a fright."

Granice was silent. He would have liked to reaffirm his guilt, to produce the fresh arguments which had occurred to him since his last talk with the physician; but he feared his eagerness might be taken for a symptom of derangement, and he affected to smile away Dr. Stell's allusion.

"You think, then, it's a case of brain-fag, nothing more?"

"Nothing more. And I should advise you to knock off tobacco. You smoke a good deal, don't you?"

He developed his treatment, recommending massage, gymnastics, travel, or any form of diversion that did not, that in short

Granice interrupted him impatiently. "Oh, I loathe all that, and I'm sick of travelling."

"H'm. Then some larger interest, politics, reform, philanthropy? Something to take you out of yourself."

"Yes. I understand," said Granice wearily.

"Above all, don't lose heart. I see hundreds of cases like yours," the doctor added cheerfully from the threshold.

On the doorstep Granice stood still and laughed. Hundreds of cases like his, the case of a man who had committed a murder, who confessed his guilt, and whom no one would believe! Why, there had never been a case like it in the world. What a good figure Stell would have made in a play: the great alienist who couldn't read a man's mind any better than that!

Granice saw huge comic opportunities in the type.

But as he walked away, his fears dispelled, the sense of listlessness returned on him. For the first time since his avowal to Peter Ascham he found himself without an occupation, and understood that he had been carried through the past weeks only by the necessity of constant action. Now his life had once more become a stagnant backwater, and as he stood on the street corner watching the tides of traffic sweep by, he asked himself despairingly how much longer he could endure to float about in the sluggish circle of his consciousness.

The thought of self-destruction recurred to him; but again his flesh recoiled. He yearned for death from other hands, but he could never take it from his own. And, aside from his insuperable physical reluctance, another motive restrained him. He was possessed by the dogged desire to establish the truth of his story. He refused to be swept aside as an irresponsible dreamer, even if he had to kill himself in the end, he would not do so before proving to society that he had deserved death from it.

He began to write long letters to the papers; but after the first had been published and commented on, public curiosity was quelled by a brief statement from the District Attorney's office, and the rest of his communications remained unprinted. Ascham came to see him, and begged him to travel. Robert Denver dropped in, and tried to joke him out of his delusion; till Granice, mistrustful of their motives, began to dread the reappearance of Dr. Stell, and set a guard on his lips. But the words he kept back engendered others and still others in his brain. His inner self became a humming factory of arguments, and he spent long hours reciting and writing down elaborate statements of his crime, which he constantly retouched and developed. Then gradually his activity languished under the lack of an audience, the sense of being buried beneath deepening drifts of indifference. In a passion of resentment he swore that he would prove himself a murderer, even if he had to commit another crime to do it; and for a sleepless night or two the thought flamed red on his darkness. But daylight dispelled it. The determining impulse was lacking and he hated too promiscuously to choose his victim. . . So he was thrown back on the unavailing struggle to impose the truth of his story. As fast as one channel closed on him he tried to pierce another through the sliding sands of incredulity. But every issue seemed blocked, and the whole human race leagued together to cheat one man of the right to die.

Thus viewed, the situation became so monstrous that he lost his last shred of self-restraint in contemplating it. What if he were really the victim of some mocking experiment, the centre of a ring of holiday-makers jeering at a poor creature in its blind dashes against the solid walls of consciousness? But, no, men were not so uniformly cruel: there were flaws in the close surface of their indifference, cracks of weakness and pity here and there. . .

Granice began to think that his mistake lay in having appealed to persons more or less familiar with his past, and to whom the visible conformities of his life seemed a final disproof of its one fierce secret deviation. The general tendency was to take for the whole of life the slit seen between the blinders of habit: and in his walk down that narrow vista Granice cut a correct enough figure. To a vision free to follow his whole orbit his story would be more intelligible: it would be easier to convince a chance idler in the street than the trained intelligence hampered by a sense of his antecedents. This idea shot up in him with the tropic luxuriance of each new seed of thought, and he began to walk the streets, and to frequent out-of-the-way chop-houses and bars in his search for the impartial stranger to whom he should disclose himself.

At first every face looked encouragement; but at the crucial moment he always held back. So much was at stake, and it was so essential that his first choice should be decisive. He dreaded stupidity, timidity, intolerance. The imaginative eye, the furrowed brow, were what he sought. He must reveal himself only to a heart versed in the tortuous motions of the human will; and he began to hate the dull benevolence of the average face. Once or twice, obscurely, allusively, he made a beginning, once sitting down at a man's side in a basement chop-house, another day approaching a lounger on an east-side wharf. But in both cases the premonition of failure checked him on the brink of avowal. His dread of being taken for a man in the clutch of a fixed idea gave him an unnatural keenness in reading the expression of his interlocutors, and he had provided himself in advance with a series of verbal alternatives, trap-doors of evasion from the first dart of ridicule or suspicion.

He passed the greater part of the day in the streets, coming home at irregular hours, dreading the silence and orderliness of his apartment, and the critical scrutiny of Flint. His real life was spent in a world so remote from this familiar setting that he sometimes had the mysterious sense of a living metempsychosis, a furtive passage from one identity to another, yet the other as unescapably himself!

One humiliation he was spared: the desire to live never revived in him. Not for a moment was he tempted to a shabby pact with existing conditions. He wanted to die, wanted it with the fixed unwavering desire which alone attains its end. And still the end eluded him! It would not always, of course, he had full faith in the dark star of his destiny. And he could prove it best by repeating his story, persistently and indefatigably, pouring it into indifferent ears, hammering it into dull brains, till at last it kindled a spark, and some one of the careless millions paused, listened, believed. . .

It was a mild March day, and he had been loitering on the westside docks, looking at faces. He was becoming an expert in physiognomies: his eagerness no longer made rash darts and awkward recoils. He knew now the face he needed, as clearly as if it had come to him in a vision; and not till he found it would he speak. As he walked eastward through the shabby reeking streets he had a premonition that he should find it that morning. Perhaps it was the promise of spring in the air, certainly he felt calmer than for many days. . .

He turned into Washington Square, struck across it obliquely, and walked up University Place. Its heterogeneous passers always allured him, they were less hurried than in Broadway, less enclosed and classified than in Fifth Avenue. He walked slowly, watching for his face.

At Union Square he felt a sudden relapse into discouragement, like a votary who has watched too long for a sign from the altar. Perhaps, after all, he should never find his face. . . The air was languid, and he felt tired. He walked between the bald grass-plots and the twisted trees, making for an empty seat. Presently he passed a bench on which a girl sat alone, and something as definite as the twitch of a cord made him stop before her. He had never dreamed of telling his story to a girl, had hardly looked at the women's faces as they passed. His case was man's work: how could a woman help him? But this girl's face was extraordinary, quiet and wide as a clear evening sky. It suggested a hundred images of space, distance, mystery, like ships he had seen, as a boy, quietly berthed by a familiar wharf, but with the breath of far seas and strange harbours in their shrouds. . . Certainly this girl would understand. He went up to her quietly, lifting his hat, observing the forms, wishing her to see at once that he was "a gentleman."

"I am a stranger to you," he began, sitting down beside her, "but your face is so extremely intelligent that I feel. . . I feel it is the face I've waited for . . . looked for everywhere; and I want to tell you"

The girl's eyes widened: she rose to her feet. She was escaping him!

In his dismay he ran a few steps after her, and caught her roughly by the arm.

"Here, wait, listen! Oh, don't scream, you fool!" he shouted out.

He felt a hand on his own arm; turned and confronted a policeman. Instantly he understood that he was being arrested, and something hard within him was loosened and ran to tears.

"Ah, you know, you know I'm guilty!"

He was conscious that a crowd was forming, and that the girl's frightened face had disappeared. But what did he care about her face? It was the policeman who had really understood him. He turned and followed, the crowd at his heels. . .

VII

In the charming place in which he found himself there were so many sympathetic faces that he felt more than ever convinced of the certainty of making himself heard.

It was a bad blow, at first, to find that he had not been arrested for murder; but Ascham, who had come to him at once, explained that he needed rest, and the time to "review" his statements; it appeared that reiteration had made them a little confused and contradictory. To this end he had willingly acquiesced in his removal to a large quiet establishment, with an open space and trees about it, where he had found a number of intelligent companions, some, like himself, engaged in preparing or reviewing statements of their cases, and others ready to lend an interested ear to his own recital.

For a time he was content to let himself go on the tranquil current of this existence; but although his auditors gave him for the most part an encouraging attention, which, in some, went the length of really brilliant and helpful suggestion, he gradually felt a recurrence of his old doubts. Either his hearers were not sincere, or else they had less power to aid him than they boasted. His interminable conferences resulted in nothing, and as the benefit of the long rest made itself felt, it produced an increased mental lucidity which rendered inaction more and more unbearable. At length he discovered that on certain days visitors from the outer world were admitted to his retreat; and he wrote out long and logically constructed relations of his crime, and furtively slipped them into the hands of these messengers of hope.

This occupation gave him a fresh lease of patience, and he now lived only to watch for the visitors' days, and scan the faces that swept by him like stars seen and lost in the rifts of a hurrying sky.

Mostly, these faces were strange and less intelligent than those of his companions. But they represented his last means of access to the world, a kind of subterranean channel on which he could set his "statements" afloat, like paper boats which the mysterious current might sweep out into the open seas of life.

One day, however, his attention was arrested by a familiar contour, a pair of bright prominent eyes, and a chin insufficiently shaved. He sprang up and stood in the path of Peter McCarren.

The journalist looked at him doubtfully, then held out his hand with a startled deprecating, "Why?"

"You didn't know me? I'm so changed?" Granice faltered, feeling the rebound of the other's wonder.

"Why, no; but you're looking quieter, smoothed out," McCarren smiled.

"Yes: that's what I'm here for, to rest. And I've taken the opportunity to write out a clearer statement"

Granice's hand shook so that he could hardly draw the folded paper from his pocket. As he did so he noticed that the reporter was accompanied by a tall man with grave compassionate eyes. It came to Granice in a wild thrill of conviction that this was the face he had waited for. . .

"Perhaps your friend, he is your friend? would glance over it, or I could put the case in a few words if you have time?" Granice's voice shook like his hand. If this chance escaped him he felt that his last hope was gone. McCarren and the stranger looked at each other, and the former glanced at his watch.

"I'm sorry we can't stay and talk it over now, Mr. Granice; but my friend has an engagement, and we're rather pressed"

Granice continued to proffer the paper. "I'm sorry, I think I could have explained. But you'll take this, at any rate?"

The stranger looked at him gently. "Certainly, I'll take it." He had his hand out. "Good-bye."

"Good-bye," Granice echoed.

He stood watching the two men move away from him through the long light hall; and as he watched them a tear ran down his face. But as soon as they were out of sight he turned and walked hastily toward his room, beginning to hope again, already planning a new statement.

Outside the building the two men stood still, and the journalist's companion looked up curiously at the long monotonous rows of barred windows.

"So that was Granice?"

"Yes, that was Granice, poor devil," said McCarren.

"Strange case! I suppose there's never been one just like it? He's still absolutely convinced that he committed that murder?"

"Absolutely. Yes."

The stranger reflected. "And there was no conceivable ground for the idea? No one could make out how it started? A quiet conventional sort of fellow like that, where do you suppose he got such a delusion? Did you ever get the least clue to it?"

McCarren stood still, his hands in his pockets, his head cocked up in contemplation of the barred windows. Then he turned his bright hard gaze on his companion.

"That was the queer part of it. I've never spoken of it, but I did get a clue."

"By Jove! That's interesting. What was it?"

McCarren formed his red lips into a whistle. "Why, that it wasn't a delusion."

He produced his effect, the other turned on him with a pallid stare.

"He murdered the man all right. I tumbled on the truth by the merest accident, when I'd pretty nearly chucked the whole job."

"He murdered him - murdered his cousin?"

"Sure as you live. Only don't split on me. It's about the queerest business I ever ran into. . . do about it? Why, what was I to do? I couldn't hang the poor devil, could I? Lord, but I was glad when they collared him, and had him stowed away safe in there!"

The tall man listened with a grave face, grasping Granice's statement in his hand.

"Here, take this; it makes me sick," he said abruptly, thrusting the paper at the reporter; and the two men turned and walked in silence to the gates.

The Gerrard Street Mystery by John Charles Dent

I

My name is William Francis Furlong. My occupation is that of a commission merchant, and my place of business is on St. Paul Street, in the City of Montreal. I have resided in Montreal ever since shortly after my marriage in 1862, to my cousin, Alice Playter, of Toronto. My name may not be familiar to the present generation of Torontonians, though I was born in Toronto, and passed the early years of my life there. Since the days of my youth my visits to the Upper Province have been few, and, with one exception, very brief; so that I have doubtless passed out of the remembrance of many persons with whom I was once on terms of intimacy. Still, there are several residents of Toronto whom I am happy to number among my warmest personal friends at the present day. There are also a good many persons of middle age, not in Toronto only, but scattered here and there throughout various parts of Ontario, who will have no difficulty in recalling my name as that of one of their fellow-students at Upper Canada College. The name of my late uncle, Richard Yardington, is of course well known to all old residents of Toronto, where he spent the last thirty-two years of his life. He settled there in the year 1829, when the place was still known as Little York. He opened a small store on Yonge Street, and his commercial career was a reasonably prosperous one. By steady degrees the small store developed into what, in those times, was regarded as a considerable establishment. In the course of years the owner acquired a competency, and in 1854 retired from business altogether. From that time up to the day of his death he lived in his own house on Gerrard Street.

After mature deliberation, I have resolved to give to the Canadian public an account of some rather singular circumstances connected with my residence in Toronto. Though repeatedly urged to do so, I have hitherto refrained from giving any extended publicity to those circumstances, in consequence of my inability to see any good to be served thereby. The only person, however, whose reputation can be injuriously affected by the details has been dead for some years. He has left behind him no one whose feelings can be shocked by the disclosure, and the story is in itself sufficiently remarkable to be worth the telling. Told, accordingly, it shall be; and the only fictitious element introduced into the narrative shall be the name of one of the persons most immediately concerned in it.

At the time of taking up his abode in Toronto, or rather in Little York, my uncle Richard was a widower, and childless; his wife having died several months previously. His only relatives on this side of the Atlantic were two maiden sisters, a few years younger than himself He never contracted a second matrimonial alliance, and for some time after his arrival here his sisters lived in his house, and were dependent upon him for support. After the lapse of a few years both of them married and settled down in homes of their own. The elder of them subsequently became my mother. She was left a widow when I was a mere boy, and survived my father only a few months. I was an only child, and as my parents had been in humble circumstances, the charge of my maintenance devolved upon my uncle, to whose kindness I am indebted for such educational training as I have received. After sending me to school and college for several years, he took me into his store, and gave me my first insight into commercial life. I lived with him, and both then and always received at his hands the kindness of a father, in which light I eventually almost came to regard him. His younger sister, who was married to a watchmaker called Elias Playter, lived at Quebec from the time of her marriage until her death, which took place in 1846. Her husband had been unsuccessful in business, and was moreover of dissipated habits. He was left with one child, a daughter, on his hands; and as my uncle was averse to the idea of his sister's child remaining under the control of one so unfit to provide for her welfare, he proposed to adopt the little girl as his own. To this proposition Mr. Elias Playter readily assented, and little Alice was soon domiciled with her uncle and myself in Toronto.

Brought up, as we were, under the same roof, and seeing each other every day of our lives, a childish attachment sprang up between my cousin Alice and myself. As the years rolled by, this attachment ripened into a tender affection, which eventually resulted in an engagement between us. Our engagement was made with the full and cordial approval of my uncle, who did not share the prejudice entertained by many persons against marriage between cousins. He stipulated, however, that our marriage should be deferred until I had seen somewhat more of the world, and until we had both reached an age when we might reasonably be presumed to know our own minds. He was also, not unnaturally, desirous that before taking upon myself the responsibility of marriage I should give some evidence of my ability to provide for a wife, and for other contingencies usually consequent upon matrimony. He made no secret of his intention to divide his property between Alice and myself at his death; and the fact that no actual division would be necessary in the event of our marriage with each other was doubtless one reason for his ready acquiescence in our engagement. He was, however, of a vigorous constitution, strictly regular and methodical in all his habits, and likely to live to an advanced age. He could hardly be called parsimonious, but, like most men who have successfully fought their own way through life, he was rather fond of authority, and little disposed to divest himself of his wealth until he should have no further occasion for it. He expressed his willingness to establish me in business, either in Toronto or elsewhere, and to give me the benefit of his experience in all mercantile transactions.

When matters had reached this pass I had just completed my twenty-first year, my cousin being three years younger. Since my uncle's retirement I had engaged in one or two little speculations on my own account, which had turned out fairly successful, but I had not devoted myself to any regular or fixed pursuit. Before any definite arrangements had been concluded as to the course of my future life, a circumstance occurred which seemed to open a way for me to turn to good account such mercantile talent as I possessed. An old friend of my uncle's opportunely arrived in Toronto from Melbourne, Australia, where, in the course of a few years, he had risen from the position of a junior clerk to that of senior partner in a prominent commercial house. He painted the land of his adoption in glowing colours, and assured my uncle and myself that it presented an inviting field for a young man of energy and business capacity, more especially if he had a small capital at his command. The matter was carefully debated in our domestic circle. I was naturally averse to a separation from Alice, but my imagination took fire at Mr. Redpath's glowing account of his own splendid success. I pictured myself returning to Canada after an absence of four or five years with a mountain of gold at my command, as the result of my own energy and acuteness. In imagination, I saw myself settled down with Alice in a palatial mansion on Jarvis Street, and living in affluence all the rest of my days. My uncle bade me consult my own judgement in the matter, but rather encouraged the idea than otherwise. He offered to advance me £500, and I had about half that sum as the result of my own speculations. Mr. Redpath, who was just about returning to Melbourne, promised to aid me to the extent of his power with his local knowledge and advice. In less than a fortnight from that time he and I were on our way to the other side of the globe.

We reached our destination early in the month of September, 1857. My life in Australia has no direct bearing upon the course of events to be related, and may be passed over in a very few words. I engaged in various enterprises, and achieved a certain measure of success. If none of my ventures proved eminently prosperous, I at least met with no serious disasters. At the end of four years, that is to say, in September, 1861, I made up my account with the world, and found I was worth ten thousand dollars. I had, however, become terribly homesick, and longed for the termination of my voluntary exile. I had, of course, kept up a regular correspondence with Alice and Uncle Richard, and of late they had both pressed me to return home. "You have enough", wrote my uncle, "to give you a start in Toronto, and I see no reason why Alice and you should keep apart any longer. You will have no housekeeping expenses, for I intend you to live with me. I am getting old, and shall be glad of your companionship in my declining years. You will have a comfortable home while I live, and when I die you will get all I have between you. Write as soon as you receive this, and let us know how soon you can be here, the sooner the better."

The letter containing this pressing invitation found me in a mood very much disposed to accept it. The only enterprise I had on hand which would be likely to delay me was a transaction in wool, which, as I believed, would be closed by the end of January or the beginning of February. By the first of March I should certainly be in a condition to start on my homeward voyage, and I determined that my departure should take place about that time. I wrote both to Alice and my uncle, apprising them of my intention, and announcing my expectation to reach Toronto not later than the middle of May.

The letters so written were posted on the 19th of September, in time for the mail which left on the following day. On the 27th, to my huge surprise and gratification, the wool transaction referred to was unexpectedly concluded, and I was at liberty, if so disposed, to start for home by the next fast mail steamer, the Southern Cross, leaving Melbourne on the 11th of October. I was so disposed, and made my preparations accordingly. It was useless, I reflected, to write to my uncle or to Alice, acquainting them with the change in my plans, for I should take the shortest route home, and should probably be in Toronto as soon as a letter could get there. I resolved to telegraph from New York, upon my arrival there, so as not to take them altogether by surprise.

The morning of the 11th of October found me on board the Southern Cross, where I shook hands with Mr. Redpath and several other friends who accompanied me on board for a last farewell. The particulars of the voyage to England are not pertinent to the story, and may be given very briefly. I took the Red Sea route, and arrived at Marseilles about two o'clock in the afternoon of the 29th of November. From Marseilles I travelled by rail to Calais, and so impatient was I to reach my journey's end without loss of time, that I did not even stay over to behold the glories of Paris. I had a commission to execute in London, which, however, delayed me there only a few hours, and I hurried down to Liverpool, in the hope of catching the Cunard Steamer for New York. I missed it by about two hours, but the Persia was detailed to start on a special trip to Boston the following day. I secured a berth, and at eight o'clock the next morning steamed out of the Mersey on my way homeward.

The voyage from Liverpool to Boston consumed fourteen days. All I need say about it is, that before arriving at the latter port I formed an intimate acquaintance with one of the passengers, Mr. Junius H. Gridley, a Boston merchant, who was returning from a hurried business trip to Europe. He was, and is, a most agreeable companion. We were thrown together a good deal during the voyage, and we then laid the foundation of a friendship which has ever since subsisted between us. Before the dome of the State House loomed in sight he had extracted a promise from me to spend a night with him before pursuing my journey. We landed at the wharf in East Boston on the evening of the 17th of December, and I accompanied him to his house on West Newton Street, where I remained until the following morning. Upon consulting the time-table, we found that the Albany express would leave at 11:30 A.M. This left several hours at my disposal, and we sallied forth immediately after breakfast to visit some of the lions of the American Athens.

In the course of our peregrinations through the streets, we dropped into the post office, which had recently been established in the Merchants' Exchange Building, on State Street. Seeing the countless piles of mail-matter, I jestingly remarked to my friend that there seemed to be letters enough there to go around the whole human family. He replied in the same mood, whereupon I banteringly suggested the probability that among so many letters, surely there ought to be one for me.

"Nothing more reasonable," he replied. "We Bostonians are always bountiful to strangers. Here is the General Delivery, and here is the department where letters addressed to the Furlong family are kept in stock. Pray inquire for yourself."

The joke I confess was not a very brilliant one; but with a grave countenance I stepped up to the wicket and asked the young lady in attendance:

"Anything for W. F. Furlong?"

She took from a pigeon-hole a handful of correspondence, and proceeded to run her eye over the addresses. When about half the pile had been exhausted she stopped, and propounded the usual inquiry in the case of strangers:

"Where do you expect letters from?"

"From Toronto," I replied.

To my no small astonishment she immediately handed me a letter, bearing the Toronto post-mark. The address was in the peculiar and well-known handwriting of my uncle Richard.

Scarcely crediting the evidence of my senses I tore open the envelope, and read as follows:

"Toronto, 9th December, 1861.

"MY DEAR WILLIAM: I am so glad to know that you are coming home so much sooner than you expected when you wrote last, and that you will eat your Christmas dinner with us. For reasons which you will learn when you arrive, it will not be a very merry Christmas at our house, but your presence will make it much more bearable than it would be without you. I have not told Alice that you are coming. Let it be a joyful surprise for her, as some compensation for the sorrows she has had to endure lately. You needn't telegraph. I will meet you at the GWR station.

"Your affectionate uncle,

"RICHARD YARDINGTON."

"Why, what's the matter?" asked my friend, seeing the blank look of surprise on my face. "Of course the letter is not for you; why on earth did you open it?"

"It is for me," I answered. "See here, Gridley, old man; have you been playing me a trick? If you haven't, this is the strangest thing I ever knew in my life."

Of course he hadn't been playing me a trick. A moment's reflection showed me that such a thing was impossible. Here was the envelope with the Toronto postmark of the 9th of December, at which time he had been with me on board the Persia, on the Banks of Newfoundland. Besides, he was a gentleman, and would not have played so poor and stupid a joke upon a guest. And, to put the matter beyond all possibility of doubt, I remembered that I had never mentioned my cousin's name in his hearing.

I handed him the letter. He read it carefully through twice over, and was as much mystified at its contents as myself; for during our passage across the Atlantic I had explained to him the circumstance under which I was returning home.

By what conceivable means had my uncle been made aware of my departure from Melbourne? Had Mr. Redpath written to him, as soon as I acquainted that gentleman with my intentions? But even if such were the case, the letter could not have left before I did, and could not possibly have reached Toronto by the 9th of December. Had I been seen in England by some one who knew me, and had not one written from there? Most unlikely; and even if such a thing had happened, it was impossible that the letter could have reached Toronto by the 9th. I need hardly inform the reader that there was no telegraphic communication at that time. And how could my uncle know that I would take the Boston route? And if he had known, how could he foresee that I would do anything so absurd as to call at the Boston post office and inquire for letters? "I will meet you at the GWR station." How was he to know by what train I would reach Toronto unless I notified him by telegraph? And that he expressly stated to be unnecessary.

We did no more sight-seeing. I obeyed the hint contained in the letter, and sent no telegram. My friend accompanied me down to the Boston and Albany station, where I waited in feverish impatience for the departure of the train. We talked over the matter until 11:30, in the vain hope of finding some clue to the mystery. Then I started on my journey. Mr. Gridley's curiosity was aroused, and I promised to send him an explanation immediately upon my arrival at home.

No sooner had the train glided out of the station than I settled myself in my seat, drew the tantalizing letter from my pocket, and proceeded to read and re-read it again and again. A very few perusals sufficed to fix its contents in my memory, so that I could repeat every word with my eyes shut. Still I continued to scrutinize the paper, the penmanship, and even the tint of the ink. For what purpose, do you ask? For no purpose, except that I hoped, in some mysterious manner, to obtain more light on the subject. No light came, however. The more I scrutinized and pondered, the greater was my mystification. The paper was a simple sheet of white letter-paper, of the kind ordinarily used by my uncle in his correspondence. So far as I could see, there was nothing peculiar about the ink. Anyone familiar with my uncle's writing could have sworn that no hand but his had penned the lines His well-known signature, a masterpiece of involved hieroglyphics, was there in all its indistinctness, written as no one but himself could ever have written it. And yet, for some unaccountable reason, I was half disposed to suspect forgery. Forgery! What nonsense. Anyone clever enough to imitate Richard Yardington's handwriting would have employed his talents more profitably than indulging in a mischievous and purposeless jest. Not a bank in Toronto but would have discounted a note with that signature affixed to it.

Desisting from all attempts to solve these problems, I then tried to fathom the meaning of other points in the letter. What misfortune had happened to mar the Christmas festivities at my uncle's house? And what could the reference to my cousin Alice's sorrows mean? She was not ill. That, I thought, might be taken for granted. My uncle would hardly have referred to her illness as "one of the sorrows she had to endure lately". Certainly, illness may be regarded in the light of a sorrow; but "sorrow" was not precisely the word which a straightforward man like Uncle Richard would have applied to it. I could conceive of no other cause of affliction in her case. My uncle was well, as was evinced by his having written the letter, and by his avowed intention to meet me at the station. Her father had died long before I started for Australia. She had no other near relation except myself, and she had no cause for anxiety, much less for "sorrow", on my account. I thought it singular, too, that my uncle, having in some strange manner become acquainted with my movements, had withheld the knowledge from Alice. It did not square with my preconceived ideas of him that he would derive any satisfaction from taking his niece by surprise.

All was a muddle together, and as my temples throbbed with the intensity of my thoughts, I was half disposed to believe myself in a troubled dream from which I should presently awake. Meanwhile, on glided the train.

A heavy snow-storm delayed us for several hours, and we reached Hamilton too late for the mid-day express for Toronto. We got there, however, in time for the accommodation leaving at 3:15 P.M., and we would reach Toronto at 5:05. I walked from one end of the train to the other in hopes of finding some one I knew, from whom I could make enquiries about home. Not a soul. I saw several persons whom I knew to be residents of Toronto, but none with whom I had ever been personally acquainted, and none of them would be likely to know anything about my uncle's domestic arrangements. All that remained to be done under these circumstances was to restrain my curiosity as well as I could until reaching Toronto. By the by, would my uncle really meet me at the station, according to his promise? Surely not. By what means could he possibly know that I would arrive by this train? Still, he seemed to have such accurate information respecting my proceedings that there was no saying where his knowledge began or ended. I tried not to think about the matter, but as the train approached Toronto my impatience became positively feverish in its intensity. We were not more than three minutes behind time, as we glided in font of the Union Station I passed out on to the platform of the car, and peered intently through the darkness. Suddenly my heart gave a great bound. There, sure enough, standing in front of the door of the waiting-room, was my uncle, plainly discernible by the fitful glare of the overhanging lamps. Before the train came to a stand-still, I sprang from the car and advanced towards him. He was looking out for me, but his eyes not being as young as mine, he did not recognize me until I grasped him by the hand. He greeted me warmly, seizing me by the waist, and almost raising me from the ground. I at once noticed several changes in his appearance; changes for which I was wholly unprepared. He had aged very much since I had last seen him, and the lines about his mouth had deepened considerably The iron-grey hair which I remembered so well had disappeared; its place being supplied with a new and rather dandified-looking wig. The old-fashioned great-coat which he had worn ever since I could remember, had been supplanted by a modern frock of spruce cut, with seal-skin collar and cuffs. All this I noticed in the first hurried greetings that passed between us.

"Never mind your luggage, my boy," he remarked. "Leave it till tomorrow, when we will send down for it. If you are not tired we'll walk home instead of taking a cab. I have a good deal to say to you before we get there."

I had not slept since leaving Boston, but was too much excited to be conscious of fatigue, and as will readily be believed, I was anxious enough to hear what he had to say. We passed from the station, and proceeded up York Street, arm in arm.

"And now, Uncle Richard," I said, as soon as we were well clear of the crowd, "keep me no longer in suspense. First and foremost, is Alice well?"

"Quite well, but for reasons you will soon understand, she is in deep grief. You must know that"

"But," I interrupted, "tell me, in the name of all that's wonderful, how you knew I was coming by this train; and how did you come to write me at Boston?"

Just then we came to the corner of Front Street, where was a lamp-post. As we reached the spot where the light of the lamp was most brilliant, he turned half round, looked me full in the face, and smiled a sort of wintry smile. The expression of his countenance was almost ghastly.

"Uncle," I quickly said, "What's the matter? Are you not well?"

"I am not as strong as I used to be, and I have had a good deal to try me of late. Have patience and I will tell you all. Let us walk more slowly, or I shall not finish before we get home. In order that you may clearly understand how matters are, I had better begin at the beginning, and I hope you will not interrupt me with any questions till I have done. How I knew you would call at the Boston post office, and that you would arrive in Toronto by this train, will come last in order. By the by, have you my letter with you?"

"The one you wrote to me at Boston? Yes, here it is," I replied, taking it from my pocket-book.

"Let me have it."

I handed it to him, and he put it into the breast pocket of his inside coat. I wondered at this proceeding on his part, but made no remark upon it.

We moderated our pace, and he began his narration. Of course I don't pretend to remember his exact words, but they were to this effect. During the winter following my departure to Melbourne, he had formed the acquaintance of a gentleman who had then recently settled in Toronto. The name of this gentleman was Marcus Weatherley, who had commenced business as a wholesale provision merchant immediately upon his arrival, and had been engaged in it ever since. For more than three years the acquaintance between him and my uncle had been very slight, but during the last summer they had had some real-estate transactions together, and had become intimate. Weatherley, who was comparatively a young man and unmarried, had been invited to the house on Gerrard Street, where he had more recently become a pretty frequent visitor. More recently still, his visits had become so frequent that my uncle suspected him of a desire to be attentive to my cousin, and had thought proper to enlighten him as to her engagement with me. From that day his visits had been voluntarily discontinued. My uncle had not given much consideration to the subject until a fortnight afterwards, when he had accidentally become aware of the fact that Weatherley was in embarrassed circumstances.

Here my uncle paused in his narrative to take a breath. He then added, in a low tone, and putting his mouth almost close to my ear:

"And, Willie, my boy, I have at last found out something else. He has forty-two thousand dollars falling due here and in Montreal within the next ten days, and he has forged my signature to acceptances for thirty-nine thousand seven hundred and sixteen dollars and twenty-four cents."

Those to the best of my belief, were his exact words. We had walked up York Street to Queen, and then had gone down Queen to Yonge, when we turned up the east side on our way homeward. At the moment when the last words were uttered we had got a few yards north of Crookshank Street, immediately in front of a chemist's shop which was, I think, the third house from the corner. The window of this shop was well lighted, and its brightness was reflected on the sidewalk in front. Just then, two gentlemen walking rapidly in the opposite direction to that we were taking brushed by us; but I was too deeply absorbed in my uncle's communication to pay much attention to passers-by. Scarcely had they passed, however, ere one of them stopped and exclaimed:

"Surely that is Willie Furlong!"

I turned, and recognized Johnny Gray, one of my oldest friends. I relinquished my uncle's arm for a moment, and shook hands with Gray, who said:

"I am surprised to see you. I heard only a few days ago, that you were not to be here till next spring."

"I am here," I remarked, "somewhat in advance of my own expectations." I then hurriedly enquired after several of our common friends, to which enquiries he briefly replied.

"All well," he said; "but you are in a hurry, and so am I. Don't let me detain you. Be sure and look in on me tomorrow. You will find me at the old place, in the Romain Buildings."

We again shook hands, and he passed on down the street with the gentleman who accompanied him. I then turned to re-possess myself of my uncle's arm. The old gentleman had evidently walked on, for he was not in sight. I hurried along, making sure of overtaking him before reaching Gould Street, for my interview with Gray had occupied barely a minute. In another minute I was at the corner of Gould Street. No signs of Uncle Richard. I quickened my pace to a run, which soon brought me to Gerrard Street. Still no signs of my uncle. I had certainly not passed him on my way, and he could not have got farther on his homeward route than here. He must have called in at one of the stores; a strange thing for him to do under the circumstances. I retraced my steps all the way to the front of the chemist's shop, peering into every window and doorway as I passed along. No one in the least resembling him was to be seen.

I stood still for a moment, and reflected. Even if he had run at full speed, a thing most unseemly for him to do, he could not have reached the corner of Gerrard Street before I had done so. And what should he run for? He certainly did not wish to avoid me, for he had more to tell me before reaching home. Perhaps he had turned down Gould Street. At any rate, there was no use waiting for him. I might as well go home at once. And I did.

Upon reaching the old familiar spot, I opened the gate, passed on up the steps to the front door, and rang the bell. The door was opened by a domestic who had not formed part of the establishment in my time, and who did not know me; but Alice happened to be passing through the hall, and heard my voice as I inquired for Uncle Richard. Another moment and she was in my arms. With a strange foreboding at my heart I noticed that she was in deep mourning. We passed into the dining-room, where the table was laid for dinner.

"Has Uncle Richard come in?" I asked, as soon as we were alone. "Why did he run away from me?"

"Who?" exclaimed Alice, with a start; "what do you mean, Willie? Is it possible you have not heard?"

"Heard what?"

"I see you have not heard," she replied. "Sit down, Willie, and prepare yourself for painful news. But first tell me what you meant by saying what you did just now, who was it that ran away from you?"

"Well, perhaps I should hardly call it running away, but he certainly disappeared most mysteriously, down here near the corner of Yonge and Crookshank Streets."

"Of whom are you speaking?"

"Of Uncle Richard, of course."

"Uncle Richard! The corner of Yonge and Crookshank Streets! When did you see him there?"

"When? A quarter of an hour ago. He met me at the station and we walked up together till I met Johnny Gray. I turned to speak to Johnny for a moment, when"

"Willie, what on earth are you talking about? You are labouring under some strange delusion. Uncle Richard died of apoplexy more than six weeks ago, and lies buried in St. James's Cemetery."

II

I don't know how long I sat there, trying to think, with my face buried in my hands. My mind had been kept on a strain during the last thirty hours, and the succession of surprises to which I had been subjected had temporarily paralyzed my faculties. For a few moments after Alice's announcement I must have been in a sort of stupor. My imagination, I remember, ran riot about everything in general, and nothing in particular. My cousin's momentary impression was that I had met with an accident of some kind, which had unhinged my brain. The first distinct remembrance I have after this is, that I suddenly awoke from my stupor to find Alice kneeling at my feet, and holding me by the hand. Then my mental powers came back to me, and I recalled all the incidents of the evening.

"When did uncle's death take place?" I asked.

"On the 3rd of November, about four o'clock in the afternoon. It was quite unexpected, though he had not enjoyed his usual health for some weeks before. He fell down in the hall, just as he was returning from a walk, and died within two hours. He never spoke or recognized anyone after his seizure."

"What has become of his old overcoat?" I asked.

"His old overcoat, Willie, what a question?" replied Alice, evidently thinking that I was again drifting back into insensibility.

"Did he continue to wear it up to the day of his death?" I asked.

"No. Cold weather set in very early this last fall, and he was compelled to don his winter clothing earlier than usual. He had a new overcoat made within a fortnight before he died. He had it on at the time of his seizure. But why do you ask?"

"Was the new coat cut by a fashionable tailor, and had it a fur collar and cuffs?"

"It was cut at Stovel's, I think. It had a fur collar and cuffs."

"When did he begin to wear a wig?"

"About the same time that he began to wear his new overcoat. I wrote you a letter at the time, making merry over his youthful appearance and hinting, of course only in jest, that he was looking out for a young wife. But you surely did not receive my letter. You must have been on your way home before it was written."

"I left Melbourne on the 11th of October. The wig, I suppose, was buried with him?"

"Yes."

"And where is the overcoat?"

"In the wardrobe upstairs, in uncle's room."

"Come and show it to me."

"I led the way upstairs, my cousin following. In the hall of the first floor we encountered my old friend Mrs. Daly, the housekeeper. She threw up her hands in surprise at seeing me. Our greeting was very brief; I was too intent on solving the problem which had exercised my mind ever since receiving the letter at Boston, to pay much attention to anything else. Two words, however, explained to her where we were going, and at our request she accompanied us. We passed into my uncle's room. My cousin drew the key of the wardrobe from a drawer where it was kept, and unlocked the door. There hung the overcoat. A single glance was sufficient. It was the same.

The dazed sensation in my head began to make itself felt again. The atmosphere of the room seemed to oppress me, and closing the door of the wardrobe, I led the way downstairs again to the dining-room, followed by my cousin. Mrs. Daly had sense enough to perceive that we were discussing family matters, and retired to her own room.

I took my cousin's hand in mine, and asked:

"Will you tell me what you know of Mr. Marcus Weatherley?"

This was evidently another surprise for her. How could I have heard of Marcus Weatherley? She answered, however, without hesitation:

"I know very little of him. Uncle Richard and he had some dealings a few months since, and in that way he became a visitor here. After a while he began to call pretty often, but his visits suddenly ceased a short time before uncle's death. I need not affect any reserve with you. Uncle Richard thought he came after me, and gave him a hint that you had a prior claim. He never called afterwards. I am rather glad that he didn't, for there is something about him that I don't quite like. I am at a loss to say what the something is; but his manner always impressed me with the idea that he was not exactly what he seemed to be on the surface. Perhaps I misjudged him. Indeed, I think I must have done so, for he stands well with everybody, and is highly respected."

I looked at the clock on the mantelpiece. It was ten minutes to seven. I rose from my seat.

"I will ask you to excuse me for an hour or two, Alice. I must find Johnny Gray."

"But you will not leave me, Willie, until you have given me some clue to your unexpected arrival, and to the strange questions you have been asking? Dinner is ready, and can be served at once. Pray don't go out again till you have dined."

She clung to my arm. It was evident that she considered me mad, and thought it probable that I might make away with myself. This I could not bear. As for eating any dinner, that was simply impossible in my then frame of mind, although I had not tasted food since leaving Rochester. I resolved to tell her all. I resumed my seat. She placed herself on a stool at my feet, and listened while I told her all that I have set down as happening to me subsequently to my last letter to her from Melbourne.

"And now, Alice, you know why I wish to see Johnny Gray."

She would have accompanied me, but I thought it better to prosecute my inquiries alone. I promised to return sometime during the night, and tell her the result of my interview with Gray. That gentleman had married and become a householder on his own account during my absence in Australia. Alice knew his address, and gave me the number of his house, which was on Church Street. A few minutes' rapid walking brought me to his door. I had no great expectation of finding him at home, as I deemed it probable he had not returned from wherever he had been going when I met him; but

I should be able to find out when he was expected, and would either wait or go in search of him. Fortune favoured me for once, however; he had returned more than an hour before. I was ushered into the drawing-room, where I found him playing cribbage with his wife.

"Why, Willie," he exclaimed, advancing to welcome me, "this is kinder than I expected. I hardly looked for you before tomorrow. All the better; we have just been speaking of you. Ellen, this is my old friend, Willie Furlong, the returned convict, whose banishment you have so often heard me deplore."

After exchanging brief courtesies with Mrs. Gray, I turned to her husband.

"Johnny, did you notice anything remarkable about the old gentleman who was with me when we met on Yonge Street this evening?"

"Old gentleman! who? There was no one with you when I met you."

"Think again. He and I were walking arm in arm, and you had passed us before you recognized me, and mentioned my name."

He looked hard in my face for a moment, and then said positively:

"You are wrong, Willie. You were certainly alone when we met. You were walking slowly, and I must have noticed if anyone had been with you."

"It is you who are wrong," I retorted, almost sternly. "I was accompanied by an elderly gentleman, who wore a great coat with fur collar and cuffs, and we were conversing earnestly together when you passed us."

He hesitated an instant, and seemed to consider, but there was no shade of doubt on his face.

"Have it your own way, old boy," he said. "All I can say is, that I saw no one but yourself, and neither did Charley Leitch, who was with me. After parting from you we commented upon your evident abstraction, and the sombre expression of your countenance, which we attributed to your having only recently heard of the sudden death of your Uncle Richard. If any old gentleman had been with you we could not possibly have failed to notice him."

Without a single word by way of explanation or apology, I jumped from my seat, passed out into the hall, seized my hat, and left the house.

III

Out into the street I rushed like a madman, banging the door after me I knew that Johnny would follow me for an explanation, so I ran like lightning round the next corner, and thence down to Yonge Street. Then I dropped into a walk, regained my breath, and asked myself what I should do next.

Suddenly I bethought me of Dr. Marsden, an old friend of my uncle's. I hailed a passing cab, and drove to his house. The doctor was in his consultation-room, and alone.

Of course he was surprised to see me, and gave expression to some appropriate words of sympathy at my bereavement. "But how is it that I see you so soon?" he asked, "I understood that you were not expected for some months to come."

Then I began my story, which I related with great circumstantiality of detail, bringing it down to the moment of my arrival at his house. He listened with the closest attention, never interrupting me by a single exclamation until I had finished. Then he began to ask questions, some of which I thought strangely irrelevant.

"Have you enjoyed your usual good health during your residence abroad?"

"Never better in my life. I have not had a moment's illness since you last saw me."

"And how have you prospered in your business enterprises?"

"Reasonably well; but pray doctor, let us confine ourselves to the matter in hand. I have come for friendly, not professional, advice."

"All in good time, my boy," he calmly remarked. This was tantalizing. My strange narrative did not seem to have disturbed his serenity in the least degree.

"Did you have a pleasant passage?" he asked, after a brief pause. "The ocean, I believe, is generally rough at this time of year."

"I felt a little squeamish for a day or two after leaving Melbourne," I replied, "but I soon got over it, and it was not very bad even while it lasted. I am a tolerably good sailor."

"And you have had no special ground of anxiety of late? At least not until you received this wonderful letter", he added, with a perceptible contraction of his lips, as though trying to repress a smile.

Then I saw what he was driving at.

"Doctor," I exclaimed, with some exasperation in my tone, "pray dismiss from your mind the idea that what I have told you is the result of diseased imagination. I am as sane as you are. The letter itself affords sufficient evidence that I am not quite such a fool as you take me for."

"My dear boy, I don't take you for a fool at all, although you are a little excited just at present. But I thought you said you returned the letter to, ahem, your uncle."

For a moment I had forgotten that important fact. But I was not altogether without evidence that I had not been the victim of a disordered brain. My friend Gridley could corroborate the receipt of the letter and its contents. My cousin could bear witness that I had displayed an acquaintance with facts which I would not have been likely to learn from anyone but my uncle. I had referred to his wig and overcoat, and had mentioned to her the name of Mr. Marcus Weatherley, a name which I had never heard before in my life. I called Dr. Marsden's attention to these matters, and asked him to explain them if he could.

"I admit", said the doctor, "that I don't quite see my way to a satisfactory explanation just at present. But let us look the matter squarely in the face. During an acquaintance of nearly thirty years, I always found your uncle a truthful man, who was cautious enough to make no statements about his neighbours that he was not able to prove. Your informant, on the other hand, does not seem to have confined himself to facts. He made a charge of forgery against a gentleman whose moral and commercial integrity are unquestioned by all who know him. I know Marcus Weatherley pretty well, and am not disposed to pronounce him a forger and a scoundrel upon the unsupported evidence of a shadowy old gentleman who appears and disappears in the most mysterious manner, and who cannot be laid hold of and held responsible for his slanders in a court of law. And it is not true, as far as I know and believe, that Marcus Weatherley is embarrassed in his circumstances. Such confidence have I in his solvency and integrity that I would not be afraid to take up all his outstanding paper without asking a question. If you will make inquiry, you will find that my opinion is shared by all the bankers in the city. And I have no hesitation in saying that you will find no acceptances with your uncle's name to them, either in this market or elsewhere."

"That I will try to ascertain tomorrow," I replied. "Meanwhile, Dr. Marsden, will you oblige your old friend's nephew by writing to Mr. Junius Gridley, and asking him to acquaint you with the contents of the letter, and the circumstances under which I received it?"

"It seems an absurd thing to do," he said, "but I will if you like. What shall I say?" and he sat down at his desk to write the letter.

It was written in less than five minutes. It simply asked for the desired information, and requested an immediate reply. Below the doctor's signature I added a short postscript in these words:

"My story about the letter and its contents is discredited. Pray answer fully, and at once. W.F.F."

At my request the doctor accompanied me to the post office, on Toronto Street, and dropped the letter into the box with his own hands. I bade him good night, and repaired to the Rossin House. I did not feel like encountering Alice again until I could place myself in a more satisfactory light before her. I despatched a messenger to her with a short note stating that I had not discovered anything important, and requesting her not to wait up for me. Then I engaged a room and went to bed.

But not to sleep. All night long I tossed about from one side of the bed to the other; and at daylight, feverish and unrefreshed, I strolled out. I returned in time for breakfast, but ate little or nothing. I longed for the arrival of ten o'clock, when the banks would open.

After breakfast I sat down in the reading-room of the hotel, and vainly tried to fix my attention upon the local columns of the morning's paper. I remember reading over several items time after time, without any comprehension of their meaning. After that I remember nothing.

Nothing? All was blank for more than five weeks. When consciousness came back to me I found myself in bed in my own old room, in the house on Gerrard Street, and Alice and Dr. Marsden were standing by my bedside.

No need to tell how my hair had been removed, nor about the bags of ice that had been applied to my head. No need to linger over any details of the "pitiless fever that burned in my brain". No need, either, to linger over my progress back to convalescence, and thence to complete recovery. In a week from the time I have mentioned, I was permitted to sit up in bed, propped up by a mountain of pillows. My impatience would brook no further delay, and I was allowed to ask questions about what had happened in the interval which had elapsed since my overwrought nerves gave way under the prolonged strain upon them. First, Junius Gridley's letter in reply to Dr. Marsden was placed in my hands. I have it still in my possession, and I transcribe the following copy from the original now lying before me:

"Boston, Dec. 22nd, 1861.

"DR. MARSDEN:

"In reply to your letter, which has just been received, I have to say that Mr. Furlong and myself became acquainted for the first time during our recent passage from Liverpool to Boston, in the Persia, which arrived here Monday last. Mr. Furlong accompanied me home, and remained until Tuesday morning, when I took him to see the Public Library, the State House, the Athenaeum, Faneuil Hall, and other points of interest. We casually dropped into the post office, and he remarked upon the great number of letters there. At my instigation, made, of course, in jest, he applied at the General Delivery for letters for himself. He receive one bearing the Toronto post-mark. He was naturally very much surprised at receiving it, and was not less so at its contents. After reading it he handed it to me, and I also read it carefully. I cannot recollect it word for word, but it professed to come from "his affectionate uncle, Richard Yardington". It expressed pleasure at his coming home sooner than had been anticipated, and hinted in rather vague terms at some calamity. He referred to a lady called Alice, and stated that she had not been informed of Mr. Furlong's intended arrival. There was something too, about his presence at home being a recompense to her for recent grief which she had sustained. It also expressed the writer's intention to meet his nephew at the Toronto railway station upon his arrival, and stated that no telegram need be sent. This, as nearly as I can remember, was about all there was in the letter. Mr. Furlong professed to recognize the handwriting as his uncle's. It was a cramped hand, not easy to read, and the signature was so peculiarly formed that I was hardly able to decipher it. The peculiarity consisted of the extreme irregularity in the formation of the letters, no two of which were of equal size; and capitals were interspersed promiscuously, more especially throughout the surname.

"Mr. Furlong was much agitated by the contents of the letter, and was anxious for the arrival of the time of his departure. He left by the B. & A. train at 11:30. This is really all I know about the matter, and I have been anxiously expecting to hear from him ever since he left. I confess that I feel curious, and should be glad to hear from him, that is, of course, unless something is involved which it would be impertinent for a comparative stranger to pry into.

"Yours, &c.,
"JUNIUS H. GRIDLEY.

So that my friend has completely corroborated my account, so far as the letter was concerned. My account, however, stood in no need of corroboration, as will presently appear.

When I was stricken down, Alice and Dr. Marsden were the only persons to whom I had communicated what my uncle had said to me during our walk from the station. They both maintained silence in the matter, except to each other. Between themselves, in the early days of my illness, they discussed it with a good deal of feeling on each side. Alice implicitly believed my story from first to last. She was wise enough to see that I had been made acquainted with matters that I could not possibly have learned through any ordinary channels of communication. In short, she was not so enamoured of professional jargon as to have lost her common sense. The doctor, however, with the mole-blindness of many of his tribe, refused to believe. Nothing of this kind had previously come within the range of his own experience, and it was therefore impossible. He accounted for it all upon the hypothesis of my impending fever. He is not the only physician who mistakes cause for effects, and vice versa.

During the second week of my prostration, Mr. Marcus Weatherley absconded. This event so totally unlooked for by those who had had dealings with him, at once brought his financial condition to light. It was found that he had been really insolvent for several months past. The day after his departure a number of his acceptances became due. These acceptances proved to be four in number, amounting to exactly thirty-two thousand dollars. So that that part of my uncle's story was confirmed. One of the acceptances was payable in Montreal, and was for $2,283.76. The other three were payable at different banks in Toronto. These last had been drawn at sixty days, and each of them bore a signature presumed to be that of Richard Yardington. One of them was for $8,972.11; another was for $10,114.63; and the third and last was for $20,629.50. A short sum in simple addition will show us the aggregate of these three amounts

```
$  8,972.11
   10,114.63
   20,629.50
$39,716.24
```

which was the amount for which my uncle claimed that his name had been forged.

Within a week after these things came to light a letter addressed to the manager of one of the leading banking institutions of Toronto arrived from Mr. Marcus Weatherley. He wrote from New York, but stated that he should leave there within an hour from the time of posting his letter. He voluntarily admitted having forged the name of my uncle to the three acceptances above referred to and entered int other details about his affairs, which, though interesting enough to his creditors at that time, would have no special interest to the public at the present day. The banks where the acceptances had been discounted were wise after the fact, and detected numerous little details wherein the forged signatures differed from the genuine signatures of my Uncle Richard. In each case they pocketed the loss and held their tongues, and I dare say they will not thank me for calling attention to the matter, even at this distance of time.

There is not much more to tell. Marcus Weatherley, the forger, me his fate within a few days after writing his letter from New York. He took passage at New Bedford, Massachusetts, in a sailing vessel called the Petrel bound for Havana. The Petrel sailed from port on the 12th of January, 1862, and went down in mid-ocean with all hands on the 23rd of the same month. She sank in full sight of the captain and crew of the City of Baltimore (Inman Line), but the hurricane prevailing was such that the latter were unable to render any assistance, or to save one of the ill-fated crew from the fury of the waves.

At an early stage in the story I mentioned that the only fictitious element should be the name of one of the characters introduced. The name is that of Marcus Weatherley himself. The person whom I had so designated really bore a different name, one that is still remembered by scores of people in Toronto. He has paid the penalty of his misdeeds, and I see nothing to be gained by perpetuating them in connection with his own proper name. In all other particulars the foregoing narrative is as true as a tolerably retentive memory has enabled me to record it.

I don't propose to attempt any psychological explanation of the events here recorded, for the very sufficient reason that only one explanation is possible. The weird letter and its contents, as has been seen, do not rest upon my testimony alone. With respect to my walk from the station with Uncle Richard, and the communication made by him to me, all the details are as real to my mind as any other incidents of my life. The only obvious deduction is, that I was made the recipient of a communication of the kind which the world is accustomed to regard as supernatural.

Mr. Owen's publishers have my full permission to appropriate this story in the next edition of his "Debatable Land between this World and the Next". Should they do so, their readers will doubtless be favoured with an elaborate analysis of the facts, and with a pseudo-philosophic theory about spiritual communion with human beings. My wife, who is an enthusiastic student of electro-biology, is disposed to believe that Weatherley's mind, overweighted by the knowledge of his forgery, was in some occult manner, and unconsciously to himself, constrained to act upon my own senses. I prefer, however, simply to narrate the facts. I may or may not have my own theory about those facts. The reader is at perfect liberty to form one of his own if he so pleases. I may mention that Dr. Marsden professes to believe to the present day that my mind was disordered by the approach of the fever which eventually struck me down, and that all I have described was merely the result of what he, with delightful periphrasis, calls "an abnormal condition of the system, induced by causes too remote for specific diagnosis".

It will be observed that, whether I was under an hallucination or not, the information supposed to be derived from my uncle was strictly accurate in all its details. The fact that the disclosure subsequently became unnecessary through the confession of Weatherley does not seem to me to afford any argument for the hallucination theory. My uncle's communication was important at the time when it was given to me; and we have no reason for believing that "those who are gone before" are universally gifted with a knowledge of the future.

It was open to me to make the facts public as soon as they became known to me, and had I done so, Marcus Weatherley might have been arrested and punished for his crime. Had not my illness supervened, I think I should have made discoveries in the course of the day following my arrival in Toronto which would have led to his arrest.

Such speculations are profitless enough, but they have often formed the topic of discussion between my wife and myself. Gridley, too, wherever he pays us a visit, invariably revives the subject, which he long ago christened "The Gerrard Street Mystery", although it might just as correctly be called "The Yonge Street Mystery", or, "The Mystery of the Union Station". He has urged me a hundred times over to publish the story; and now, after all these years, I follow his counsel, and adopt his nomenclature in the title.